TALES FROM THE RED ROSE INN
AND OTHER PLAYS

by
Don Nigro

SAMUEL FRENCH, INC.
45 WEST 25TH STREET   NEW YORK 10010
7623 SUNSET BOULEVARD   HOLLYWOOD 90046
LONDON   TORONTO

IMPORTANT BILLING AND CREDIT REQUIREMENTS

CONTENTS

TALES FROM
THE RED ROSE INN

CHARACTERS

Susannah Rose
James Armitage

SETTING

A bed in an upstairs room of the
Red Rose Inn, in Armitage, Ohio,
in the year 1779.

TALES FROM THE RED ROSE INN

(Sound of crickets in the darkness. Lights up on SUSANNAH
ROSE, age 17, huddled in her nightgown on a bed in the
upstairs room of the Red Rose Inn in Armitage, Ohio, little
more than a cabin in the wilderness, in the year 1779. James
Armitage, age 35, stands near the edge of the light, look-
ing at her.)

SUSANNAH. In a throw of dice. As if I were some animal.

JAMES. You are an animal, and a lovely young animal at
that, and, lucky for us, so am I. A game of chance is simply a
metaphor. So is this place, for that matter. It stands for what
it's not.

SUSANNAH. What?

JAMES. Hell is a metaphor, and so is paradise. They're the
same place, actually, as God and his opposite are most likely
the same imaginary personage, wearing different masks.

SUSANNAH. Don't stand there and speak blasphemies to
me. You're the opposite of God. You and my drunken father,
like a couple of savages. Playing at dice for the flesh of his
daughter. It isn't enough to have lost his house and his land,
so he gambles away his daughter's flesh to a stranger.

JAMES. That's not an entirely accurate description of
what's happened. In the first place, it wasn't his land, it was
my land. He was just squatting on it. I think it was awfully

7

sporting of me to give him a chance to keep it, playing at dice, under the circumstances, when I might just as easily have cut his throat.

SUSANNAH. And what would you have done if he'd won?

JAMES. Cut his throat.

SUSANNAH. And taken me by force?

JAMES. You're better off with me than him in any case. He lost you in a game of chance. I would never do that.

SUSANNAH. You won me in a game of chance, but you wouldn't risk me in another?

JAMES. I wouldn't lose.

SUSANNAH. You're a horrible, horrible man.

JAMES. Well, yes, I am, but then again, as horrible men go, I'm probably the best you're going to run across in this godforsaken place, so we might as well make the best of it.

SUSANNAH. I don't understand what you're even doing here. Why are you here? Is it because you killed someone?

JAMES. Who told you that?

SUSANNAH. You did, when you were drinking with my father. I heard you say you killed someone in Boston.

JAMES. And you believed me?

SUSANNAH. About that, yes.

JAMES. Well, it's as good a reason as any. Why is anybody anywhere? Why are you here?

SUSANNAH. I had no choice. My father brought me here. We're not the sort of people who belong anywhere.

JAMES. Nobody belongs anywhere, as far as that goes, but this is as good a place as any to die in.

SUSANNAH. If you've come here to die, then my advice is, do it and get it over with.

JAMES. That's it. Pretend you don't like me. But we know better, don't we?

SUSANNAH. You think I like you? I hate you.

JAMES. You don't know me.

SUSANNAH. I don't want to know you. And I don't even think James Armitage is your real name.

JAMES. What's wrong with my name? It's an excellent name.

SUSANNAH. You wear it like ill-fitting clothing. When people call out your name, you don't answer at first. It's as if you need a moment to remember that's who you are.

JAMES. What difference should it make to you what my name is? If you don't like this one, I'll make up another.

SUSANNAH. Whoever you think you are or pretend you are, I won't be bought and sold.

JAMES. I didn't buy you. I won you.

SUSANNAH. I am not a creature to be owned.

JAMES. I don't think I own you. What I won, as I understand it, is this place, which I already had to begin with, and your father's permission to take you if I can persuade you to have me, which I didn't need in the first place. If you don't want to be here, you're quite free to go.

SUSANNAH. Just where the hell am I supposed to go? We're in the middle of deeply wooded godforsaken nowhere. And this is the only place that's ever felt like home to me. I have no other place. It's this place, or die in those woods. It's more my place than yours.

JAMES. No it's not. I bought it from the Delawares, although in point of fact I believe the Delawares fairly recently stole it from somebody else. You might just as well say it belongs to the animals, or the trees. It belongs to whatever lives here. In the matter of geography, at least, possession is everything. And in other matters as well.

SUSANNAH. Well, you are never going to possess me, whatever your name is. I'd rather die.

JAMES. You'd rather die than be with me?

SUSANNAH. I'd rather die than be traded like a horse from one man to the next.

JAMES. Look about you, child. This is a cruel place. There's the war. We're not even supposed to be on this side of the Ohio. But restless, lost white people are forever creeping in like some disease that murders the trees. I know what we are.

I know we've come here to kill this place, whatever else we think we're doing here. I can't help that. I've come from a worse place than this, and I'm sick to death of other people. It's time I came to rest.

SUSANNAH. Then why don't you just put a gun to your head and pull the trigger?

JAMES. Tried that once. Didn't go off. My powder was wet.

SUSANNAH. A man with any real character wouldn't give up so easily.

JAMES. That's why all the men with character are dead and buried. I myself have come to the conclusion, after some serious soul searching and a good deal of hard drinking, that on the whole I prefer you to blowing my brains out. I mean to stay and run the Red Rose Inn, and I have full confidence that you will be the chief attraction here.

SUSANNAH. Is that it, then? Do you mean to set me up for a whore?

JAMES. No. I mean to set you up for my wife.

SUSANNAH. Your wife? Your wife?

JAMES. If you want to stay here, it only makes sense for us to marry. If you don't love me now, you will soon enough. You hate me already, and that's a good start.

SUSANNAH. Do you think I would ever be wife to a man like you?

JAMES. I don't see why not. Women have chosen much worse men for no apparent reason.

SUSANNAH. And the Delawares had no business selling you anything, because this land actually belongs to a man named Christopher Rumpley.

JAMES. Christopher Rumpley?

SUSANNAH. Yes. I expect him to come and claim it any day now.

JAMES. What do you know about Christopher Rumpley?

SUSANNAH. I know his claim to this land is carved on the big oak tree in the back garden.

JAMES. I'm sorry to have to report to you that Christopher Rumpley is dead.

SUSANNAH. Dead?

JAMES. I'm afraid so.

SUSANNAH. Christopher Rumpley is dead?

JAMES. I take it from the stricken look on your face that Christopher Rumpley was a close friend of yours.

SUSANNAH. Yes. Well, no. I never actually met him. But I felt very close to him. You're absolutely certain he's dead?

JAMES. I have it on very good authority.

SUSANNAH. Oh.

JAMES. If those tears are for him, they're the first anybody's shed on his behalf.

SUSANNAH. So, basically, nobody owns this place?

JAMES. Nobody owns anything. We must live somewhere. This is the place we're at. It's mine until somebody takes it from me, and that's highly unlikely.

SUSANNAH. If you only have it on good authority, then you don't actually know for certain that he's dead. How can you be sure he won't return one day and gut you like a deer?

JAMES. I know he's dead because I killed him.

SUSANNAH. You killed him?

JAMES. I did.

SUSANNAH. You killed Christopher Rumpley?

JAMES. I must confess, yes. Now, would you like your honeymoon before or after the wedding?

SUSANNAH. You beast. You hideous, hideous beast. You cheerfully inform me you've murdered my friend Christopher Rumpley and you expect me to marry you?

JAMES. Ridding the world of Christopher Rumpley was a pure act of mercy on my part, both for him and the world. The man wanted me to kill him.

SUSANNAH. I don't believe that.

JAMES. Oh, yes. He'd lived far too long. I did him a great kindness. I'll probably go to heaven for it. Can we get married now? I've hog-tied a preacher in the potato cellar, and I'd really like to sleep with you tonight.

SUSANNAH. Just what do you think I am? The village idiot?

JAMES. No, I don't think you can properly be called the village idiot when we have no village yet.

SUSANNAH. Of course we have no village. We have nothing. I have nothing. I'm sitting here, lost in a game of chance, lost before that really, in the middle of nowhere—

JAMES. As opposed where?

SUSANNAH. As opposed to somewhere.

JAMES. And where exactly is somewhere?

SUSANNAH. Not here.

JAMES. Trust me, Susannah, I've been to that unjustly celebrated location, somewhere, and returned to tell the tale, and the essence of the tale is, it feels as much like nowhere when you're somewhere as it does anywhere else. All places on earth are stolen places. All places are scenes of murder and betrayal. We're all murderers or the children of murderers, and our children will be murderers as well. There's theft and murder built into the fabric of the universe. Ripeness is all.

SUSANNAH. You're beginning to make me envy Christopher Rumpley. I think he's in a better place than I.

JAMES. No, you don't want to envy that poor son of a bitch. Believe me, I knew him as well as any man could. I buried him with my own two hands in the back garden of Mrs Turley's Bunch of Grapes in Boston, Massachusetts, and, trust me, my dear, Christopher Rumpley was not a man any sane person would care to envy, let alone stumble across in the dark.

SUSANNAH. So you were a friend of his, were you? Before you did him the favor of murdering him?

JAMES. You seem awfully interested in this Rumpley person, for a fellow you never actually met. A man could almost be jealous. What could that hopeless ruffian possibly have meant to you?

SUSANNAH. When we first came to this place, I found that tree with his name carved in it, Christopher Rumpley,

January, 1761. And then beneath that, Christopher Rumpley, his land, October 1763. Just that. An old Delaware woman told me she remembered a big, strange young man carving marks in that oak tree, and then returning two years later with some other white men, and buying the land from the old chief who lived here, and carving more marks on the tree. It made a strong impression on her because she said it was bad luck to carve in a tree, disrespectful to the spirit of the woods. I used to lie under the tree and look up at those carvings. It was like a message to me in a private code, a secret promise of some sort. I'd imagine Christopher Rumpley coming back to claim his land, or maybe taking me away someplace. I don't know. It was a foolish thing, but it's all I had, and now you've murdered him, and I've nothing else to hope for.

(SUSANNAH begins to sob, softly and with great dignity.)

JAMES. Are you weeping again, Miss Rose?

SUSANNAH. Get away from me.

JAMES. I wish you wouldn't.

SUSANNAH. I don't care what you wish. Why should you mind if I weep? Am I not even allowed my own tears? Do you think you own them, too?

JAMES. I'm annoyed that you're shedding tears for a man you only knew by a name carved twice in a tree sixteen or eighteen years ago. It's a waste of perfectly good body fluids, and I find it frankly incomprehensible that you would mourn so terribly for a dead stranger rotting in a Boston garden.

SUSANNAH. I'm mourning for myself.

JAMES. Oh, Miss Rose, you're a pathetic mess when you cry. It is really not a thing I wish to look at on an empty stomach.

SUSANNAH. Then go away.

JAMES. *(Sitting down on the bed beside her.)* Tears shed for Christopher Rumpley. What an extraordinary thing. I'll tell you what I can about him if you like. He was through here with Colonel Rogers, on the way back from Detroit. That's when he first set eyes on this place and carved his name so he'd know it again when he returned. Because he knew he would return. Something about this place just felt to him like the place he was going to die in. I don't know why. I don't think he could have explained it himself. Like most true things, it made no sense whatsoever. Then, two years later, he was back, with Colonel Bouquet, and they camped near here, and he found the tree and bought the land from an old Delaware chief who thought him a great fool to believe that land could be bought and sold like women. Then he went back to Boston and loved a girl who went mad, not because he loved her but for another reason, and then rather to his surprise, after a time he loved another girl, and fathered a child upon her, and then he murdered a man who sold oysters, and grew sick of the revolution, the butchery and posturing and hypocrisy of it, and decided he'd used up his life, and one dark night, when we were pretending to be quite drunk, he asked me, as his only friend on earth, if I wouldn't mind doing away with him once and for all, to put an end to his suffering, and so I obliged him, for compassion's sake, as he really was a miserable wretch, and in his dying gratitude he told me to come and claim his land, which I have done, and here I am, sitting on a bed with a beautiful woman, and wanting to comfort her so badly I think I will lose my mind if I don't, and watching her cry because the man I killed is dead. The wages of compassion is frustration.

SUSANNAH. So he was wrong about this being the place he was to die in.

JAMES. I thought the least I could do was come here and die in it for him.

SUSANNAH. In short, first you murdered him, and then you stole his land.

JAMES. You miss the point entirely if you feel sorry for him. He was a lost soul at best. When he was a boy he's stowed away on a boat from London. His father was an actor who longed for a more respectable life, and so became a thief and was subsequently hung for it. His greatest performance, the boy thought. Then he watched his mother die of consumption, decided he'd seen enough of London, stole passage on a boat to Boston, joined up with Rogers' Rangers, fought at Ticonderoga, and came, in the twisted course of time, to this fateful place, and knew it, with the certainty of his own particular madness, to have a powerful private meaning for him. Sometimes a piece of land or a woman will just strike a man that way.

SUSANNAH. Why did he want to die?

JAMES. How can I look into another's soul?

SUSANNAH. You know. You know why he wanted to die. Tell me.

JAMES. He wanted to die because he hadn't met you.

SUSANNAH. Ballocks.

JAMES. He wanted to die because he'd loved three women in his life. The first was dead, the second mad, and the third tried to murder him during an act of sexual congress.

SUSANNAH. No. Women die for men now and then, but men seldom die for women. And why this place? What was so special about this particular place?

JAMES. This place is the center of the universe.

SUSANNAH. This is not the center of the universe.

JAMES. It is. It only seems like nowhere to you because this is the place you happen to be. In fact, every place is the center of the universe, as long as you happen to be there, and happily for you and me, here we are.

SUSANNAH. I believe you're insane.

JAMES. I might be insane, but I'm here, which gives me a great advantage over anybody who's not, and I'm alive, another great point in my favor over your precious dead beloved Christopher Rumpley.

SUSANNAH. Just shut up and leave me alone. Can't you just leave me alone?

JAMES. You can pretend I'm your tree-carving imaginary lover if you like.

SUSANNAH. Pretend? I don't want to pretend anything any more. What good has pretending ever done anybody? Pretending is for fools and lunatics.

JAMES. And actors. Don't forget actors.

SUSANNAH. Aren't they all the same thing?

JAMES. I see you know your Shakespeare.

SUSANNAH. What about him?

JAMES. The lunatic, the lover and the poet
are of imagination all compact.

SUSANNAH. Are you quoting Shakespeare at me?

JAMES. My father was an unsuccessful actor and an even less successful thief. They hung him for the latter, although the former has at various times in the unfortunate history of western civilization also been a capital offense. He died pretending, and left me his books, or, rather, what was left unsold of them, which was one frayed and tattered old copy of Shakespeare. The Bible he sold.

SUSANNAH. That's not your story. It's Christopher Rumpley's story. It's his father who was an actor, not yours.

JAMES. How do you know who my father was? For that matter how do you know I'm not Christopher Rumpley?

SUSANNAH. Because you're not.

JAMES. How do you know I'm not?

SUSANNAH. Because you've just got done telling me you murdered him.

JAMES. And you'd take the word of a murderer that I'm not his victim?

SUSANNAH. You're not Christopher Rumpley.

JAMES. All right, yes, but suppose I was? If I was Christopher Rumpley, do you think you could love me?

SUSANNAH. If I was a bird, I could fly.

JAMES. Unless you were a penguin.

SUSANNAH. But I'm not a penguin, and you're not Christopher Rumpley, and this is the stupidest conversation I've ever had in my life.

JAMES. You've got to work with me here, Susannah. You

fell in love with a person who only existed in your head. Why can't you simply imagine I'm him?

SUSANNAH. Because you're not him.

JAMES. Imagine I am.

SUSANNAH. I don't want to imagine you're him.

JAMES. Ah, but you see, my dear, I think you do.

SUSANNAH. No I don't.

JAMES. Suppose for a moment this. Suppose that Christopher Rumpley, sick to death of that self-righteous prig Sam Adams and his stupid revolution, and having just murdered an oyster seller for deflowering a poor sweet girl and driving her mad, and buried him in the back garden of a Boston inn and sometime brothel, and having become thoroughly disgusted with every element in his life, had decided he might as well murder himself as well, that is, close the play he's been performing in, and begin a new one as somebody else. So he takes, say, his actor father's first name, James, and his actress mother's last name, Armitage, and creates a new role for himself.

SUSANNAH. Suppose, suppose. Suppose this. Imagine that. Imagination is all a great load of ballocks.

JAMES. Imagination is all we are.

SUSANNAH. Flesh and blood is all we are.

JAMES. What we are is what is in our heads. And what is in the heads of us human creatures is imagination. It's imagination makes everything. Nobody can do anything unless some half crazy person first imagines doing it. And that is who we are. But imagination, like love, takes a certain amount of courage. Suppose you have the courage to imagine I made up the story of your lover's death, and took another name so I could escape the consequences of his treachery, his various and sundry murders, on the battlefield and off. Imagine this a winter's tale, and I your beloved come to claim you, Have the courage to take on the role I've offered you in the play of our lives.

SUSANNAH. I don't want to be in your stupid play. You're a raving lunatic.

JAMES. And pleased to be one. It's my heritage. Come and join me. Take a chance. Throw the dice with me, Susannah. You be in my play and I'll be in yours, and we'll put them together and make up the scenes as we go along. Tales From the Red Rose Inn, a play by you and me, with significant additional contributions from Indians and rattlesnakes and our shrieking menagerie of filthy, snot-nosed children. At the end of this particular scene, you and I, through the pure power and joy of our united imaginations, become one flesh.

SUSANNAH. There is no play.

JAMES. There is nothing else but the play. There is only the tale well told, or badly told, or told both well and badly, turn and turn about, world without end, amen. And when we are dead, you and I will be characters in the tales our grandchildren tell. Grandfather carved his name in a tree and then became somebody else and came to Ohio and won Grandmother in a game of chance and she surprised herself by loving him anyway. It's a damned good story, don't you think?

SUSANNAH. I don't want a story. I want a life.

JAMES. If you want a life, you must have a story, or you have nothing.

SUSANNAH. I don't want that story.

JAMES. Then make up another and we'll play that. Do you prefer the story that Christopher Rumpley is dead and I killed him?

SUSANNAH. I prefer the truth.

JAMES. You prefer to be loved, and to love the person who loves you, and to be treated decently and made to laugh when you're melancholy and held close when you're lonely and protected when you're in danger. You prefer to take care of a man when he needs you and to share and laugh and cry together, and make tender, passionate love together and eat and grieve and build and make children together and watch them grow and turn into people who make their own stories. You prefer to be alive. So be alive with me. I'm offering you the role of your life. It's the best damned role you'll ever get to play. It's got everything. Mystery, intrigue, danger, romance. What do you say, Susannah Rose? Shall we fashion together a fine winter's tale for our grandchildren? Shall we? Oh, please, shall we, you and me, together? I need so desperately to fashion this tale with you, my love.

(Pause. SUSANNAH looks at JAMES for a long moment.)

SUSANNAH. When we're alone in bed at night, in the dark, may I call you Christopher?

JAMES. When we're alone in bed at night, in the dark, my dear, you may call me anything you please.

SUSANNAH. Well. Court me a while, and we'll see.

JAMES. All right, but not too long, for life is short, and the woods is full of wolves. How shall I court you?

SUSANNAH. Tell me stories.

JAMES. All right. Once upon a time there was a man who was nobody, and a girl who was lost, and they stumbled upon one another in a dark forest, and lived very happily together for some time after.

SUSANNAH. That's a very unlikely story, Christopher.

JAMES. Yes. That's the beauty of it.

(SUSANNAH looks at him and smiles. The light fades on them and goes out.)

END OF PLAY

CHILDE ROWLAND
TO THE
DARK TOWER CAME

Childe Rowland to the dark tower came,
his word was still Fie, foh, and fum,
I smell the blood of a British man.

—fragment of a lost ancient ballad, sung by Edgar in the guise of Tom o'Bedlam in Shakespeare's *King Lear*, Act Three, Scene Four.

There they stood, ranged along the hill-sides, met
        to view the last of me, a living frame
        for one more picture! in a sheet of flame
I saw them and I knew them all. And yet
dauntless the slug-horn to my lips I set,
        and blew. "Childe Roland to the Dark Tower came."

—Robert Browning, "Childe Roland to the Dark Tower Came."

No, it is impossible; it is impossible to convey the life-sensation of any given epoch of one's existence—that which makes its truth, its meaning—its subtle and penetrating essence. It is impossible. We live, as we dream—alone ...

But his soul was mad. Being alone in the wilderness, it had looked within itself, and, by heavens! I tell you, it had gone mad. I had—for my sins, I suppose—to go through the ordeal of looking into it myself.

—Joseph Conrad, *Heart of Darkness.*

CHILDE ROWLAND TO THE
DARK TOWER CAME

(Lights up on NEFF, a man in his forties, late at night, on the stage of a theatre.)

NEFF. I can't tell you how pleased I am to welcome you here for this adjudication, and in my capacity as supreme adjudicator, I would like to take a moment to say a few words about the nature of adjudication itself, as we gather once again to adjudicate the adjudications of our fellow adjudicators. When in the course of human events it becomes necessary for one group, let's call this the chief adjudicatory group, to take it upon themselves to adjudicate the adjudications of other adjudicators, whom we will call the adjudicatees, it behooves us to elucidate what exactly distinguishes the one from the other. Could you, for example, take an adjudicator, staple a different label to his forehead, and thus magically transform him into an adjudicatee? Especially given that the steamer was sunk, the guts torn out, her cold blue eyes staring back at him, naked, accusing—

Hello? I know you're out there, somewhere in the darkness, watching me, biding your time like toads in a poisoned tank, waiting for me to let my guard down. The prince of darkness is a gentleman. I come here at night, when rehearsals are over and the students have scuttled back down the drainpipe into the sewers, and I wander through this mammoth, gray, concrete edifice, which looks, Henry said, like two gigantic

preying mantises copulating, although everything tends to put
Henry in mind of some form of copulation, a labyrinth of rooms
and corridors that open suddenly upon offices and practice
rooms and lumber rooms and costume shops and prop rooms
and concert halls and this. This theatre. My domain. I wander
down corridors and close my eyes, and when I open them, I'm
lost. I begin at curfew, and walk till the first cock, moving
inexorably into the yellow, dead in the center. I know you're
out there watching in the darkness. Have you come to me in
the guise of one of the students, Tom O'Bedlam, or that horrible
pregnant Greek exotic dancing girl? If you wish to converse
with me, why don't you just come to my office? My door is
always open, except when I'm there, but you can make an
appointment with the woman knitting at the end of the long
corridor, although it had better be pretty damned important,
because I'm a busy man, so if it's some piss-ant question about
procedures, just check your departmental handbook. You can
get a copy from Drusilla for eleven dollars and fifty-seven
cents, and everything you need to know is there, believe me. I
spent a lot of time on it, my whole life, in fact, so just buy it
and save us both the excruciating humiliation of pretending to
have a conversation. Not that I have anything to fear. My books
are in apple pie order. I have a concept, you see. The secret is
to have a concept, and, having come now at last to the dark
tower—having come now at last—

     Just what the hell is your problem, anyway? Do you have
some kind of bee up your ass about the way I'm running this
department? Because my goal is to make this the best theatre
department in the observable universe. And I think in the short
time I've been here, we've made extraordinary progress. We've
finally got all the seats bolted down in the experimental theatre, so we won't be wasting time trying to change the damned
configuration every time we do a new production. Don't get
me wrong. I'm all for experimentation, as long as we keep the
seats bolted down and follow the rules in the handbook. I'm
proud to say we've also finally got rid of the undergraduate

acting major and most of the acting classes. My feeling has always been that university theatre departments waste entirely too much time trying to teach people how to act, which is manifestly impossible, and not nearly enough on deconstructive hermeneutics. And another reform I'm very proud of is the strict limitation of rehearsal time, which will solve two problems: one, it will mean less rehearsal, which I know has been exhausting everybody around here for years, and two, since we're confining our rehearsals to the daylight hours, you'll only have time to take those courses required in the handbook, instead of screwing around with electives. This department has been turning out entirely too many actors, and if there's one thing this world does not need it's more fucking actors. What we need is deconstructive hermeneuticians. That's why I spend so many hours locked in my office, writing memorandums. A great university runs on memorandums. Memorandums are the grease upon which the system slides, and I see myself, above all else, as a magnificent system greaser. Grease is how we communicate with one another, and communication is what we're about, as long as it doesn't get out of hand. Would you very much mind letting me measure your head? The foul fiend follows me. Through the sharp hawthorn blow the cold winds. The Straw Man blows out the candle. I am a two penny half penny river steam boat with a penny whistle attached. An imposter, on a journey to the center.

I hope you're not one of those unfortunate people who's been threatening to blow up the new Fine Arts Center, because I, for one, feel that this building is a great monument to postmodern architecture, bizarre acoustics notwithstanding, and those of you who are late for your classes because you keep getting lost on the way from the parking lot should really consider changing your major to horticulture. It's true, there are very few windows, but windows only encourage people to look, and that, in my experience, is seldom a happy situation. I have a big window in my office, of course, but I've already made plans to have it bricked up. I keep getting this feeling that people are outside looking in at me while I'm sharpening my pencil. I am an emissary of light. It is my responsibility to wean those ignorant millions from their horrid ways. Hello? Are you the person who's been tap dancing in the hallway late at night? I've been chasing you down these corridors at three o'clock in the morning for months now, you son of a bitch. Is that you, Arthur? Are you the one who's been putting up crude drawings on the bulletin board of me having intercourse with Popeye? Or are you that enormously pregnant Greek exotic dancer who refused to drop out of her acting classes? It was that son of a bitch Palestrina who told you to report me to the ombudsman wasn't it? Sex discrimination my ass. What if the dean walked in and saw you eight months pregnant in a leotard standing on your head? And stop coming up to me in the hallway when I'm interviewing prospective new faculty and asking me if I want to feel the baby kick. I think that sends entirely the wrong message. This is not my concept. Aroint thee, witch. My study is how to prevent the fiend and kill vermin.

Because some persons just naturally gravitate towards the position of adjudicator, and some, for whatever reason, seem to always find themselves in the position of adjudicatee, over and over, world without end. Why is this, you ask? Well, those who waste their time deluding themselves that they're creating works of art become adjudicatees, either because of what they have done, that is, manufacture rubbish, or because of what motivates them inside, that is, a deep and powerful desire to be adjudicated. Persons of taste and discrimination, on the other hand, more often than not are forced to take on the onerous burden of becoming adjudicators, whether because their minds are more analytical, hence better equipped for adjudication, or because they simply know in their hearts that they are among that select group of individuals blessed with divine adjudicatory gifts. Intelligence, perceptiveness, strength, an absence of sentimentality, courage, an uncanny ability to zero in on weakness, this is what we find in the great adjudicators, a kind of ruthless passion for ferreting out what's inherently inferior, and for exposing impostors, fuzzy thinking, sloppy execution, all those qualities which we normally associate with the mind of the adjudicatee, who is born with a strong predisposition towards the inevitable martyrdom of the touchyfeely wishywashy nambypamby artsyfartsy. This ruthless capacity for adjudication is such a thrilling thing it makes my very nipples tingle just to think about it. And as for the grim red leer of the doppelganger one sees gazing mournfully back at one in the darkened mirror of art, this is the foul fiend Flibbertigibbet, hog in sloth, fox in stealth, wolf in greediness, dog in madness—how do you manage to keep such clean linen? The light on her face makes her look quite sinister, and how the darkness surrounds her so.

Did you hear that? I keep hearing bagpipes. I thought we got rid of all the bagpipes after my groundbreaking deconstructive hermeneutical production of the Scottish play. Just because four students were nearly decapitated in the second act doesn't mean it wasn't a wonderful production. Now I'm very much looking forward to my new adaptation of *Heart of Darkness*. I've been trying to figure out a way to do it without actors. It's not that I don't love actors. Nobody likes working with egomaniacal nymphomaniac borderline psychotics more than I do. But my job as director, as I understand it, is to create three dimensional pictures. And you've got to know your concept. Anybody who doesn't know their concept before they start should be taken out behind the power plant and shot in the head. Terence, have you been fornicating with my crash dummies again? I've been toying with the idea of creating a whole audience of crash dummies, but we have one graduate student who keeps getting emotionally involved with them. Theatre is not about emotion. Theatre is about having a fucking concept. If the actors get in the way, screw them. Just don't screw the crash dummies. In my justly celebrated production of *Woyzeck* I had a steeply raked stage covered with a gridwork of razor sharp spikes, and one or two actors did trip and impale themselves, but an actor's got to learn how to move gracefully, even in big furry costumes and German helmets. And hanging from the flies we had these giant cows that would twirl and swing back and forth when we turned on the fans. I loved watching actors try to remember their lines while teetering on that gridwork and dodging those gigantic cows, especially when the fog machine was turned on. And we did give them umbrellas to help keep their balance and deflect the ball bearings we dropped from the catwalk. So what if we lost a couple of freshmen on those spikes? There's too many actors anyway. It's like thinning the herd. There's always fifty volunteers to step up and take a dead actor's place. Do you understand what I'm trying to say? Do you see what I'm getting at here? The boat might be at the bottom of the river, but everybody who survived behaved splendidly, except for that little blond girl in Berlin who—

I heard that. Are there hyenas in this building? We've been having some problems with the natives. I know you people come here at night to fornicate in the costume shop. My wife Elsie wants us to do only good Christian theatre. Of course, Elsie is seriously demented. She believes Jesus takes baths with her. I told Henry, if this was a small Central American country, I wouldn't have to put up with all this crap. You'd have to learn Spanish, he said. No, you cretin, the point is, if this was a small Central American country, I could just have a few people taken out and shot. Elsie tells me I should pray about it. Do you think I should pray? I prayed before I went to Germany. And after. But not while I was there. It was very clean in Germany, except for the bloodstains. And out the windows of the train I could see sheep. I think people could learn a lot from sheep. Hell, people ARE sheep. Old knitter of black wool. Guarding the portcullis in the dark above Gravesend. Marshes. Forests. Savages. When I am dead they will carve my bones into dominoes. They are sneaking into the shop at night to steal wood for their productions. They are looking in the windows at me, seaweed dripping from their heads. Tempests, cold, fog, disease, exile. Armadillos skulking round the corridors. To live in the midst of the incomprehensible. Surrender to the abomination. Blue eyes of the snake in a German bar. A misunderstanding over hens. A whited sepulchre. Do I speak bad German? Do you dare to laugh at my German, here in the city of the dead? I know there is a conspiracy here to set ratsbane in my porridge. It is no good measuring my head with calipers. I was once the god of Iowa. The change has taken place inside. The whole meaning lies within the shell of a cracked nut. Ever any madness in your family? No. Just my wife. I will have my revenge ere I depart this house.

I didn't march in here, you know, like I was invading Poland. I was invited here. They invited me. They wanted me here. Gabe and Mariana. They were my old graduate students, when I was the god of corn and hogs. They made this world. But they didn't want to be in charge. They just wanted to teach and direct and talk to their stupid fucking students. I want to declare a benign anarchy, he said. It was chaos, pure chaos, when I arrived here. Old crazy Arthur tap dancing in the halls and throwing his lit cigar into waste paper baskets, his mind back in vaudeville with the Dolly Sisters. Henry Mahaffey directing his shows like a general conducting a battle he always, inevitably, lost, forever having to piss like a racehorse, with Jack Daniels in the bottom drawer. And Popeye designing sets and Olive Oyl in the costume shop. You call this a faculty? These people, I said to myself, must be dealt with. But how?

Henry has a story. He tells it at least once a week. It explains the world to him somehow. He's in the Marines and he's waiting in line to get his pay check and there's a woman standing very calmly in front of him, waiting her turn, chatting pleasantly to him, and she mentions in passing that the man at the table issuing the checks happens to be her husband, and when she gets to the head of the line, she pulls out a Luger from her handbag, says to the man behind the desk,

This is for you, you filthy son of a bitch, jams it up his nostril and pulls the trigger, and blam, his head explodes, she blows his whole face off, just like that. Brains splattered all over the place. Then she puts her gun back in her handbag, tells Henry to have a nice day and walks away. Each time I heard him telling this story, I would stick my head in his office and ask him, how's your horse, Henry? A stiff-legged, blind old horse he loved desperately. I knew the horse was dead, of course. I just liked to see the look of anguish pass across his face. And yet his story does explain the world. What I really need is a hit man.

Is it darker now? This also has been one of the dark places of the earth. Snow on the trees down the twisted streets to the campus. Ghosts in cellar caverns. There in the cemetery the dead poetess rots. An angler in the lake of darkness. Meet the nightmare. Make them squirm. Make them writhe. Make them scream. Under the knuckle. Cow dung in my mouth. Keep thy foot out of brothels. I think she is eating my brain. It seems to me I am trying to tell you a dream, making a vain attempt, because no relations of a dream can convey that commingling of absurdity, surprise, and bewilderment, that notion of being captured by the incredible which is the very essence of dreams. What's needed is a concept, not some sentimental pretense, but something you can set up, and bow down before, and offer a sacrifice to. Gabe and Mariana. Two black hens. Killed in a scuffle with the natives. Bones in the tall grass. The village abandoned. In the tropics one must before everything keep calm. An impostor on a journey to the center. I knew one who hanged himself on the side of the road to the dark tower. Bitten to death by flies. In the interior, you will no doubt meet Mr Kurtz. I'm not sure who is alive and who is not, but when one comes here, it is not to gaze at the moon. There is a physical impossibility involved in the thing. What I really want is rivets, to patch up my steamboat. You understand that I fear neither God nor Devil, let alone any mere mortal man. I saw a hippopotamus today. The porters have been trying to kill it for weeks. This animal leads a charmed life. But no man bears a charmed life. They have stolen the wood from my shop and then put it back. They are positively demonic. Mariana and Gabe. These people pretended to love me once. Now all is unspeakable desolation.

I feel as if I'm wearing somebody else's clothes. Who is the fellow in yon mirror? Blue eyes of the snake looking back at me. Somebody is always whispering around corners. Gnomes, perhaps. They bite. There are rats in my bell tower. Spear the water rat, a sound like a baby's shriek. Seldom went such grotesqueness with such woe. Bog, clay and rubble. A sordid farce acted in front of a sinister back-cloth. Faces like grotesque masks. Writhing in the extremity of an impotent despair. For her birthday I gave my wife Elsie some rope made into a noose. Do you think she would take the hint? She used it to tie up a hammock. But what if she should one day cut her throat while slicing a cucumber? Or strangle herself on piano wire while tickling the ivories in the parlor? What if she should absent-mindedly take the mixmaster with her into the tub? What? Old Elsie dead? I am shocked, shocked, do you hear? I was in my office at the time, writing memorandums to the dead. I have killed the hippopotamus at last. So this is the elephants' burial ground. I heard the truth from a hairdresser's dummy. She whispers in the costume shop at night, doing the act of darkness with an actor. Sometimes I peek at them through a small rip in the papered window. Carnivorous flies buzzing, trapped. Groans from a trucklebed. The copulations of pygmies. It is extremely difficult to guard against clerical errors in this climate. Paths twisting everywhere. A dead whore in Berlin. No, it has nothing to do with me.

And yet—and yet one must pay a price for greatness. Sometimes even the most exalted of adjudicators may find himself unexpectedly thrust into an unfamiliar position, thrown by mistake among the wretched company of adjudicatees, herded along with the filthy, the slovenly and the dispossessed, brought before a panel of adjudicators and adjudicated. But the worst case of all is to become that most grotesque of all creatures in the jungle, the adjudicator turned adjudicatee who must preside over the adjudication of his own adjudications, trapped like a fly in a webwork of complex adjudicatory molasses which—

Let's talk turkey here. I want to talk turkey. I want to make this perfectly clear. You are not my adjudicators. Let us never forget what Nietzsche said, just before his descent into godhead, he said that only God can judge me, and since I am God, only I can judge myself, and since being God I am everything, then everything judges myself, so I am judged as in a house of mirrors, with all the Corinthians looking back and shrieking at me in broken slivers of glass. Of course, in Heaven, Elsie says, all will be forgiven. Except of course for the adjudicators. The adjudicators will not be forgiven, except perhaps in Hell. Don't laugh at me. In my kingdom there is no laughter.

> One makes a magic circle on the floor
> and copulates against the green room door.

Do something that reveals your true self, I said to her. Take off your clothes. You'll never be an actress if you're ashamed to expose yourself. This is what I learned in Germany, from a small blond girl: there is no such thing as benign anarchy. You hire me to take the burden of rule off your shoulders so you can direct, so you can teach, so you can play at creation, leaving the administration, the exercise of power, to me. Well, I will take this burden from your shoulders, but do not look so shocked when I also take the opportunity to remove your head. Trust me? You trust me? How grotesquely insulting of you. I am insulted by your trust. One never respects a person one can trust. Trust is the lowest form of self-deception. No great man can be trusted. You deserve what you get. You have brought me into power in fact precisely in order to accomplish your own destruction. Here in the great theatre of the world in the bowels of the dark tower where two gigantic concrete preying mantises copulate endlessly I will take up this burden and eliminate you vermin for the good of humanity. And if there is a whore lying in a filthy hotel room in Berlin, strangled, say, with bruises upon her neck, lying naked there sprawled upon the bed like the cover of a cheap novel, I know nothing about it.

I hope I have not made you uneasy. And yet, one who inspires uneasiness can go far before he is murdered. The situation is very grave, and I am ill. I have been smelling a corpse, hidden somewhere beneath the seats, here in the dark tower. The forest spectral in the moonlight. The carcass of some dead animal. A beast with two backs. I know that goddamned Italian bastard has been sneaking into the shop at night and stealing my lumber so he can build the set for his wretched play. I know about the murder in the red barn, and the copulations below, among the caged animals and birds. Do not trust this man. They say he is a graduate student, but I know that he is Satan. He would stab you in the eyes as soon as look at you. Does he dare to assert that I have misquoted Albert Einstein? I, the toast of Wilhelmstrasse? I have not come here in this pitch blackness to gaze at the moon, like an empty biscuit tin. The great man's task is to set his face resolutely towards his station. And my station is desolate. All of my donkeys are dead. The alligators have eaten my hippos. This is an outrage. Tenured faculty do not eat one another in public. We eat one another in private. In public we chew on rotten hippo meat. Sometimes at night I go up on the catwalk to weep and howl and yank out my teeth with pliers. A madwoman from North Carolina, a lunatic from Utah, and a pack of cretinous graduate students. Who are they to challenge my wrath? I, who have created them, can destroy them. Thus sayeth the Lord God of Lamentations and greasepaint. The tap dancing, piano playing, blue eyed god who has just returned from Berlin, a divided place, with a worm in his brain. We will be all butchered in this fog. Devils gnawing at the inside of my head. Prolonged hunger. Hyenas prowling among the corpses. My shoes are full of blood. The heart of another is a dark forest. In such moments one cannot decide whether to apply to clown college or raise soybeans. A girl? Did I mention a girl? The mind of man is capable of anything, because everything is in it, the past, the future, the stench of dead hippo. The only thing to do is tip the bodies overboard. Listen to the splash in the water.

They are terrified of the steam whistle. A harlequin waving his arms like a windmill upon the shore. Palestrina, sitting in that glass office, advising the pregnant exotic dancer to go to the ombudsman, and the way she embraced me in the hallway. The little slut. She knew what she was doing. She wanted to see my face turn red. Peaches and new wine. Scarecrows. Heads on the ends of poles, staring at me. This is what we do with such people: slice them open, rip out the fetus from their steaming guts, take it between our teeth and chew and chew. There will be no disorder in my kingdom.

One can just make out dark human shapes in the distance. Is that a red light? The unseen presence of victorious corruption, like the humming of bees in a hive. I had such immense plans. I was on the threshold of great things. Words heard in dreams. Phrases spoken in nightmares. The appalling face of a glimpsed truth—the strange commingling of desire and hate. I want no more than justice. I want nothing more than fairness in this adjudication. And if a few of the natives must be sacrificed and devoured along the way, it is simply the price we pay for admission to this holy demonic pandemonium. The theatre would be such a wonderful place if only there were no people in it. This is my concept, Terence. Carve this into your forehead with your fingernails: The first thing we do is, kill all the actors. And then of course the audience. I see an audience of headless bodies, each with a small bloody piece of paper carefully pinned above the heart. Exterminate them! Exterminate all the brutes! For there is nothing more glorious in the universe than to stand alone triumphantly upon a great hillock made from the piled up carcasses of one's enemies, amid the stench of blood, and shriek out boldly and clearly one's final and irrevocable adjudication into the heart of an immense and impenetrable darkness.

(The light fades on him and goes out.)

END OF PLAY

LUCY AND
THE MYSTERY
OF THE
VINE-ENCRUSTED
MANSION

CHARACTERS

Lucy Quoit, and occult investigatrix, alias Imogen.
Diccon Mucklestane, brother to Imogen and
a barnacle fancier.
Daniel Rath, a somewhat disoriented hero.

SETTING

The rank, disturbing garden of the vine-encrusted
mansion, and certain locations within the latter. A wooden
bench amid a bit of perhaps imaginary greenery.

"I am trying to separate myself from remembrances."
—Wilkie Collins, *The Haunted Hotel.*

"It was with a great shock that she realized, whilst occupied
with extruding her antimacassar from the maid, that Herbert
was in fact not German at all. He was, remarkably,
not even Herbert."
—Janos Drago, *Fragments from an Occult Diary.*

LUCY AND THE MYSTERY OF THE
VINE-ENCRUSTED MANSION

(Sound of doves cooing in the darkness. Lights up on LUCY, a teen-age girl in a summer dress, holding a book and sitting on a bench amid tangled greenery.)

LUCY. Being, as she was, a bit fey, Lucy could tell at once that the vine-encrusted mansion was haunted. Touched with the madness of her intuitive arcane knowledge, she stood, breathless, in the tangled courtyard, heart pounding under her pertly nubile young bosoms, gazing up at the house like a virgin bride looks at her throbbing lover on their wedding night. But Lucy was not afraid, for Lucy knew no fear. Lucy was hungry for the unknown, she had an appetite for the bizarre, an unquenchable thirst for the grotesque and the outré. For Lucy was an occult investigatrix, tender in years, but fierce as a wolf and worldly wise in her ancient soul, despite the barbs and insults of her dead sister Prunella, who was a great, farting, nosepicking sow.

DICCON. *(A young man, wandering in, holding a bucket.)* Imogen? Is that you? Is somebody in the garden? *(He doesn't seem to see her, looks in the bucket.)* Come on, then, Bill. Off to the sassafras tree.

(DICCON goes out.)

LUCY. Through the broken gate she had crept. An old

brown mansion by the river, of inestimable antiquity, steep-roofed like a tower view of Rotterdam, the rank garden twined lasciviously all around it, wild, tumid sassafras trees and great reeking masses of wanton demented honeysuckle clutched into poison ivy in a passionate, deathlike embrace, fantastic paths twisted through broken fences and ruined stone walls. This was the labyrinth into which she had stumbled unawares that summer day, while contemplating her loneliness with a dog-eared copy of Balzac by her side, pondering the unexpected felicities of mistranslation.

DANIEL. *(Entering, another young man, with wire spectacles and a book.)* Imogen, it's the oddest thing. I am accompanied everywhere of late by strange narration.

(DANIEL sits beside LUCY.)

LUCY. Smell of the water, laps on the shore. Fragments of broken crockery and rusted clockworks in the weeds. Pigeons and doves in the attics.

DANIEL. I read Balzac in the garden, and hear her murmuring in my head, like pigeons and doves. Her breasts, and the smell of fresh sheets.

LUCY. Rats squeak in the dripping basements. Up from the broken windows crept the autumny apple-cellar smell. Ivy up the walls, like a girl's white arms clutched to the back of her lover as he enters in the moonlight. Snakes slide into crumbling walls. Something has happened in this place.

DANIEL. Down the twisted staircase to her bedroom. Ticking of the clock.

(He takes off his spectacles and rubs his eyes.)

LUCY. *(Putting his spectacles on.)* Nobody knows who lived in this house, or how long ago. Buzzing of flies and bees. Sound of a dead girl's pretty feet, slapping on broken cobbles on a moonlit night. They have called me a mad girl, she said, because I am fifteen and lost, but they have lied. I am not fifteen and lost. I am nearly sixteen and lost. But wise, oh, so wise for her young years. Brave Lucy. The contemplation of this ghastly disorder elicited from her virgin womb a shuddery, anticipatory fluttering. She pushed open the creaking door and stepped into the house. *(Sound of a door creaking open.)* What language do the dead speak at weddings? she asked herself. And how shall I translate this?

DANIEL. From the first moment I saw her, in her sun dress among the honeysuckle, I longed to press her naked flesh to mine.

LUCY. She stands in the dusty parlor by the cobwebbed piano, shivering in her loins, a broken rocking horse in the corner. Someone has sat here, fingering Chopin etudes in the darkness. Someone was murdered here. A naked girl, covered in blood.

DANIEL. This is the night, I said, and I am trembling. The moon coagulates. But what have I done with my spectacles?

LUCY. Now, behave yourself, young man, says the bewhiskered old fuddydud solicitor, poking about in papers and old law books, moths flying out, or I shall have my charwoman, Mrs Grimes, eat your nose.

DANIEL. This was my crypto-Dickensian inheritance: upon the unfortunate demise of my Great Aunt Peach, bless her crabby old swiss cheese soul, who died of a sneezing fit when a superfluity of moth dust caused a fatal inflammatory effulgence upon the hair follicles of her nasal passages, I, Daniel Rath, an orphan, did inherit—

LUCY. This vine-encrusted mansion, upon which lived at the time—

DANIEL. Two poor distant cousins, brother and sister, Diccon and Imogen Mucklestane.

DICCON. *(Appearing again, with pail.)* My sister Imogen and I will stay and caretake, if you like, cousin Daniel. Or go if you prefer, out into the piebald autumn. Our future disposition waits upon your kind indulgence.

LUCY. And Daniel, being by nature a generous young man—

DANIEL. Of course you must stay, cousin Diccon, you and your sister Imogen, and caretake the vine-encrusted mansion.

DICCON. You're a kind-hearted gentleman, Daniel. Isn't he, Imogen?

LUCY. He is a miracle of rare device, said Imogen. His eyes. The cooing of the doves.

DANIEL. I looked into her eyes and saw, as in a mirror—

LUCY. So Daniel let them stay, ate Diccon's horrid cooking, and cast his eye upon fair Imogen. Watch out for spiders, Daniel. The spiders will get in a person's head. And he began to notice certain odd things, in the vine-encrusted mansion.

(DICCON takes a flugelhorn from his bucket and blows a very loud and flatulent note in DANIEL's ear. DANIEL jumps.)

DICCON. Don't be alarmed, cousin Daniel. It's merely the flugelhorn with which I summon Imogen, when she is lost in the garden labyrinth. Well, I must go attend to my bubble and squeak and sassafras tea.

(DICCON goes.)

LUCY. Diccon likes you very much, said Imogen. He never blows his flugelhorn for strangers. Has he shown you his sponges yet?

DANIEL. Sponges?

LUCY. He collects sponges and barnacles in the cellars. He lives in constant apprehension that they'll crawl away. My brother is sensitive, you see. We are so grateful to you, Daniel. We feared you would evict us. The vine-encrusted mansion is all we've known, thanks to the charity of Great Aunt Peach, here at the pits of the marshmoor, by the ruins of the mucus factory. Home sweet home.

DANIEL. Has it always been just you and Diccon here?

LUCY. Oh, no. There were the twins, Mopsa and Dorcas, who died in a freak noodle accident, and Uncle Titlick, who expired of a discharge of molasses from his ear, and our sister Prunella, who ran off with an itinerant ventriloquist and choked to death on a hand puppet. I must tell you something, Daniel, said Imogen. Diccon still fears you will throw us out. He intends to employ me as a means of entanglement.

DANIEL. Entanglement?

LUCY. He hopes if you grow fond of me—

DANIEL. I assure you, dear Imogen, that's not necessary.

LUCY. Then you don't fancy me at all. I thought as much.

DANIEL. But I do fancy you. Very much. What I mean is, I have no intention—

LUCY. *(Pointing to his lap.)* What's that?

DANIEL. I beg your pardon?

LUCY. I saw something move in your lap, just to the left of your Balzac. Could it be an earwig? We are much plagued with earwigs. Or is it a crumbly bun? We're desperately hungry all the time. Great Aunt Peach didn't feed us. It's a wonder we're not cannibals. Do you like barnacles? Diccon says each barnacle has its own personality. He talks to them, and gives them all names. Bill is his favorite.

DANIEL. He gives names to barnacles?

LUCY. Sometimes at night, lying naked and alone in my chamber, I dream of my brother's barnacles, crawling up the bedpost. At such times, I wish for strong arms to hold me. I shall wish for it this night, as I lie naked and trembling all alone in Great Aunt Peach's fourposter, under the duckdown quilt. You can't imagine the loneliness, she said. I have grown so weary of imaginary love. Well, time for bed.

(She kisses him on the cheek, then rises, yawning and stretching herself most fetchingly. Sound of a ticking clock.)

DANIEL. Night, and the ticking of the clock. Fortified by

drink, I crept down the spiral staircase to her boudoir, my nostrils full of her honeysuckle perfume, thinking of how she looked standing by the piano, her thin summer dress clinging to her gently curved young fawnlike body, and how she spoke of the ghosts of dead fortune tellers, haunting the abandoned carousel by the gazebo at the back of the garden.

LUCY. Night in the vine-encrusted mansion, and my beloved descends the spiral staircase, past the ticking clock. I lie in bed and wait for his embrace, wearing only his spectacles, as I am very near-sighted, and a cross between my fair white breasts.

DANIEL. I hesitate upon the steps, heart pounding, erect as a pitchfork. Tick tock. My brain is like the clock. But something is wrong.

LUCY. Thump, thump, goes my heart. Oh, why won't he hurry? I lie here in a stupor of unrequited anticipation. My hearing is preternaturally acute. I hear mice whispering in the walls. Note to myself. Here insert the sound of mice whispering. *(Sound of mice whispering.)* I tremble so. The eyes of the dead do not stop looking at you, thought Imogen. I saw him looking at my legs. I think he will like my legs. Kissing my legs. I think that will give him some pleasure, before he dies.

DANIEL. Why do I hesitate?

LUCY. Why does he hesitate? said Imogen.

DANIEL. I hesitate because I hear a voice. I hear it everywhere. As if someone were narrating my life. Every step I take, she narrates it.

LUCY. He said, not taking any steps.

DANIEL. She narrates me as if I were the hero of some ghastly Gothic romance.

LUCY. It must be, said Lucy to herself, that the present haunts the past. She had long been aware that ghosts are prone to violent, strange hallucinations, but she'd never before encountered one who believed himself to be a character in a novel she was writing in her head.

DICCON. *(Returning, spying on DANIEL from behind the*

bench.) There he is, my little barnacle friends. There on the spiral staircase.

LUCY. I don't care if I'm in a novel or a pagoda or a pickle farm, said Imogen. I just want him to creep into my bed and make tender desperate love to me. I am feverish. My nipples squeak and bleed. I see a naked girl, covered in blood.

DICCON. Whispering on the staircase. Where is my barnacle knife?

LUCY. And she began to wonder, could the psychic powers which set her apart from others be in fact the ability to turn all experience, past, present and future, imagined and unimaginable, into a wondrous and complex labyrinth of fictions, narrative, dramatic, lyrical, and semi-lugubrious?

DICCON. *(Finding a curved, hideous looking knife in his bucket.)* Here is my barnacle knife. I keep it for cutting remarks.

LUCY. If he doesn't come soon, I'm starting without him, said Imogen. Why have the flowers withered in the rain?

DANIEL. And then he understood. He was not in love with the naked girl in the bed. He was in love with the voice in his head, the girl in his brain who narrated his life. It is the girl in my head, he said, who is my one true love.

LUCY. I'm feeling very strange today, said Lucy. I'm feeling like at least two other people.

DICCON. *(Sitting on the bench beside DANIEL and sharpening the knife on a whetstone.)* It is a courtesy to the murder victim to sharpen one's knife on a whetstone, so the barnacle knife twists firmly into the guts.

LUCY. I am entirely prepared to show this man my nipples, said Imogen, to let him suck upon my virgin nipples, to project his damp enigma into my quivering vestibule, and yet he stands there like a pork tree in a shit storm, blathering about a woman who does not exist.

DANIEL. He could see her then, quite clearly, in the parlor, by the cobwebbed old piano. She was young and innocent, and her elbows were perfectly formed. Her name was

Lucy, and she was an occult investigatrix, and the narrator of his ghostly dream.

LUCY. Lucy? said Imogen. Who the hell is Lucy?

DICCON. Well, if it's good enough for barnacles, it will do for a cousin, I think.

LUCY. It was quite disorienting for the hithertofore un-flappable Lucy Quoit to feel herself pulled inexorably into what appeared to be either someone else's haunting, or, more odd still, someone else's novel. And then it struck her, like a hail of barbells: that was the kind of haunting this was, here in the vine-encrusted mansion.

DANIEL. If I reach out, I can almost touch her breasts.

LUCY. This was the sort of haunting that sucked one deep into its own narration. The vine-encrusted mansion was a kind of living, dark, carniverous novel which sucked one in and made of one a character.

DANIEL. (Reaching out, squinting.) I can almost touch the nipples of her breasts.

LUCY. He's with another woman, said Imogen, leaping from her bed, naked as a petunia. He is touching the nipples of some slut named Lucy in the parlor.

DANIEL. You are the one I love. You are the goddess who's been writing me.

LUCY. No, said Lucy. Listen to me, ghost. You only think I am the author of your novel, when in fact all I've done is stumble unawares into your haunting. She is the one you want. Not me.

DANIEL. No. You're the one I worship. Oh, Lucy, write me, write me.

LUCY. There by the piano I see them, said Imogen.

DANIEL. One kiss. Please. Just one kiss to make you real.

LUCY. I do not wish to be real, cried Lucy. I wish to be the mistress of my own pandemonium.

DICCON. The one achievement of my life: I cut his throat with a barnacle knife.

LUCY. This is the haunting Lucy found: the brother murders

him in the sister's bed, and buries him in the garden. But the sister, naked and covered with her lover's blood, goes mad, and screams at him. Oh, cruel, cruel. He was my one true love, and you cut his throat with a barnacle knife. I hate you, she screams. You and your barnacles, too.

DICCON. She hates us, Bill. And she wears his spectacles still.

LUCY. And in despair he hangs himself from a sassafras tree, and the mad girl wanders alone in the garden, telling lurid stories to herself. Thus ends the strange tale of Lucy and the Mystery of the Vine-Encrusted Mansion. Next, the tale of Lucy and the Mystery of the Haunted Windmill.

DANIEL. No, wait. You mustn't close the book. I love you. You have written me and I love you.

LUCY. No. You are merely the echo of a wraith, she said. Whereas I am nearly sixteen and lost. And when I walk in the garden I hear voices, due to my intuitive arcane powers. One day, the beautiful occult investigatrix, Lucy Quoit, was walking by a ruined windmill, and clutching at the dog-eared, blood-splattered copy of Balzac given her by her dead lover, when she felt a violent quivering in her loins. Oh, she cried. Something has happened in this place. Someone was murdered here.

(DANIEL and DICCON look at her. The light fades on them and goes out. Sound of doves cooing in the darkness.)

END OF PLAY

DARKNESS
LIKE A DREAM

And we fairies, that do run
by the triple Hecate's team
from the presence of the sun,
following darkness like a dream ...

—*A Midsummer Night's Dream* (V.1.369-72)

For Marnie Kerby

DARKNESS LIKE A DREAM

*(DESDEMONA, a young woman, sits in a dim shaft of light.
Occasional lights pass across her, as if driving late at night,
but there is no steering wheel and she does not attempt to
mime the actions of driving.)*

DESDEMONA. Seven years I hadn't seen him, and of
course seven is a magic fairy tale number, and they say that
seven years is how long it takes for every cell in your body to
have been replaced by other cells, so he was a totally different
person, and I was a totally different person, so we didn't know
each other at all, except that the cells you are now have kept a
kind of memory of your former self, an imperfect memory,
like photocopying a page and then photocopying the photo-
copy, life is the persistence of form through the replacement
of substance, I remember that from college, some test I didn't
pass, because that's all I could remember, but that seemed to
be the only thing worth remembering.

I was being a tree fairy at the time. I wore a body stocking
and all this rather wonderful crap hanging off me like rocks
and weeds and moss and such, and my hair wild and blond
and this little forest of trees growing on my head, and I crawled
around under the steps in the moonlight and stole handker-
chiefs and spied on the young lovers sleeping in the woods. I
was the Forest of Athens, the other fairy people and I, Cob-
web and Peaseblossom and Fernface and whoever. Midsummer. A nice play. I invited him to come and he magically appeared. I never imagined he would. Seven years, and there he

49

was driving all this way out to this theatre in the woods in the middle of nowhere to watch me crawling about in the moonlight with foliage on my head. Sometimes, he said, he could only recognize me by my hands. He remembered my hands. Seven years and he remembered my hands.

And so the play is over and I'm taking a shower backstage and trying to wash the fairy makeup and the forest off my flesh, but it won't come off, it's like the forest has grown into me or something, like I'm always going to be part fairy now, and I'm scrubbing and scrubbing, and it's taking so long I'm sure he must have gone, but I come out and look up the hillside and there he is, standing by the steps, tall and strange, looking down at me, waiting for me, just for me. What does he want? Why is he here? Probably I'm dreaming.

So I walk up the steps and hug him and my heart is in my throat, I don't know what to say to him, I don't know what to do with him, and his eyes are brown like tree bark and his hands are strong on my back like vines and he smells like the woods and the night, and I ask him if he wants to go some-place and talk, and he says yes, he does, which is nice except I don't really know of anyplace, this theatre is so far out here in the middle of the woods, and he doesn't know the area, in fact he got lost on the way here, his map was wrong, and I only know the one way to get here from where I'm staying, and now it's very dark, new moon, and he's got no idea where he is or how to get home, and I have my car and he still has his big old truck thing he had seven years ago and so I say, well, why don't you just follow me, and I'll find a place for us to stop and have some coffee or something and we can talk. So he gets in his truck and I get in my car and we drive out of the parking lot and into the night, and it's very dark, it's so dark, July 23rd, new moon, and I drive off into the night, and he's following me. I lead, he follows. It's like a dream, only very dark. And I'm thinking, my God, all this time, seven years I haven't seen him, a brief hug, a few words of conversation, and then immediately I'm alone again, in my car, driving in the dark, and there he is, alone in his truck, behind me, all this time and we hardly say two words to each other and now we're alone again each of us in our cars in the darkness driving. I lead, he follows, into the darkness, like a dream.

So pretty soon I pull out onto the interstate, like I always do, because this is the way I go home, the only way I know. We always follow old paths, whether we want to or not, and there's more traffic than I thought there'd be and I realize this is not actually very easy, to keep together, me in front, him following, in the middle of the night on a dark road when he has no idea where he is and I only know the way from the theatre to where I'm staying, and at merges sometimes these stupid other cars insist on squeezing in between us, and I start to panic. I think, I'm going to lose him. I'm going to lose him forever. I just found him again after seven years when I never thought I would and I had one hug and about two minutes of nervous conversation with him and then I immediately went and lost him in the dark, these damned people for some reason have got to squeeze in between us, I hate these people, two cars, three cars, why do they need to get between us? So I slow down and they get impatient and they pass me and I look back and there he is, his headlights in my rear view mirror, following me in the dark.

And I realize, this is kind of dangerous. Trying to watch the road, watch the signs, keep track of the other cars in front of us, behind us, passing us, merging with us, getting between us. My palms are sweating. My heart is pounding. This has got to be nervewracking for him, too, trying to keep up with me, not knowing where he is or where we're going, following a girl he hasn't seen in seven years, into the dark, just these two red tail lights ahead of him in the dark. I seem to remember he can't see very well at night. What if he gets confused and ends up following the wrong car to God knows where? He's older than me. What if he drops over dead from all the excitement? Or what if he gets too close and I have to slow down suddenly and he doesn't slow down in time and we crash and burn together. I can see this in my head. I'm a nervous wreck. It's like a nightmare.

But after a bit there's less traffic, and it's mostly just us and the darkness, and I decide, well, actually, this is not so bad. This is actually kind of nice. I mean, I know exactly where he is. And I'm in control here. When I speed up, he speeds up. When I slow down, he slows down. He has no idea where I'm taking him. We're passing through unfamiliar territory. He's got to be totally lost now. I'm completely in charge of this adventure. I kind of like this. I mean, it's actually a very intimate kind of relationship, in its own way. His eyes locked on my rear end, me glancing up every few seconds to make sure he's still there. I speed up just to see him speed up. I slow down, just to feel him slow down. For a few seconds he gets too close, going too fast, and then he slows down again, keeping just the right distance, not too far away, but not too close. It's kind of like a dance. Or like this very intimate and strange, private, special form of lovemaking. I initiate. He responds. It's very nice.

I turn off the interstate and he turns off with me. Nothing is open this time of night, but by now I don't really care. This is nicer than having coffee. So I keep driving. I blink right, he blinks right. I blink left, he blinks left. I speed up, I go over the speed limit, just to see if he'll speed just to keep up with me. He does. Not only can I make him blink just by blinking, I can get him to break the law just by pressing my foot down on the accelerator. And I'm thinking, well, I could take him to that hamburger place where you eat in your car. But I'm starting to remember all the ways things never work out. I mean, right now, there's no way he can disappoint me, as long as he keeps following me. This is a very pure form of trust, he's trusting me with his life, pretty much, out here in the dark, driving and driving, on dark and narrow tree lined roads now, deep into the forest. It's a kind of test. Does he want me enough to keep following? Blind faith. What proof is there of love, really? Only a kind of blind, relentless following no matter what, into the darkness. So I decide to just keep going. If I never stop, then I'll never be hurt, he'll never disappoint me, he'll never betray me, he'll never get the chance to turn into somebody horrible like pretty much every other man I've ever known. No, this is much better. It's so intimate. So private. Just us. Deeper and deeper into the enchanted woods, the man follows the beautiful wood fairy into the dark labyrinth of the forest.

Then I realize: at some point we're going to run out of gas. One always does run out of gas eventually, doesn't one? So, what then? Well, it depends. Suppose we both happen to run out of gas at exactly the same time, which is very unlikely, I know, as you almost never finish at the same time, in my experience, but suppose we do. We both just sort of slow down and roll to a stop, in formation, until we're both there sitting in our cars by the side of the road, listening to the crickets. Somebody must get out of the car first, and walk over to the other car. But if it's me, then I cease to be in charge, because I've made the first move, I've gone back to him. And if it's him, then I also cease to be in charge, because he's made the first move. Or maybe neither one of us moves. Maybe he waits for me, and I just sit there in my car, and he just sits there waiting, and gradually my headlights burn down, and his headlights burn down, like stars burning out in some distant galaxy, and then we both just sit there in our separate cars in the darkness, me in front, him behind, and years later some kids come along and find us, two skeletons, covered in cobwebs, sitting in their cars, weeds and vines growing up through our bones.

But that's a rather unlikely scenario, in my opinion. It's much more likely that either I run out of gas first, or he does. Now, if I run out of gas first, I start to roll to a stop, he's still going, he catches up with me. Then what happens? Does he stop? Or does he keep on going, and slam right into me? No, because as I've slowed down, he has also slowed down, until his front bumper is gently nuzzling my back bumper, like sleeping with my back to him, my naked back against his naked chest, which would be very nice, except that touching, of course, is always the first step towards disaster. And if he touches me, out here in the dark, if he touches me with that bumper of his, all bets are off, and I'm lost. If he touches me, I'm lost. Of course, I'm already lost. I have no idea where I am. I've been so busy thinking about all this stuff, I've stopped looking at street signs a long time ago. I'm not sure there are any street signs any more, and I've just been driving and driving and turning randomly here and there in the dark, just so I can see his blinker come on when mine does.

And there's the other possibility, that is, that he'll run out of gas before I do, and he'll start slowing down behind me, dropping farther and farther behind me, his headlights getting dimmer and dimmer in my rear view mirror. So what do I do then? Do I stop? Do I start backing up? Do I turn around and go back to him? Because if I turn around and go back to him, then I lose control of the situation, and he'll find out that I'm just as lost as he is.

So maybe I don't stop, and I don't turn around and go back. Maybe I just keep driving. He sees my red tail lights getting farther and farther away from him, getting smaller and smaller in the darkness, and then I just vanish. And he's left there all alone in the dark. And he's lost. He's followed the fairy girl deep, deep into the labyrinth of the enchanted forest, and now he's lost there, abandoned and lost there forever. And he sits there lost in the darkness and weeps for me, but I can't hear him, because I'm gone.

That's how I'll always remember him. That's how I'll dream about him, when I'm old. The man who returned after seven years, as in a fairy tale. The only man in my whole life who never disappointed me, who never betrayed me. The only one who loved me enough to follow me, blindly and without question, into the darkness. Lost there in the dark, enchanted woods. All mine. Forever.

(The light fades on her and goes out.)

END OF PLAY

JOAN OF ARC
IN THE AUTUMN

In the years immediately following her trial,
there were many rumors that the true Joan
of Arc had not in fact been executed by the
English. In 1436, Joan's brothers announced
that she was still alive, and three years later
they came to Orleans with a young woman
they insisted was Joan.

This play is for Marnie, with deepest love.

JOAN OF ARC IN THE AUTUMN

(JOAN sits on a bench in a garden. Sound of birds.)

JOAN.
It's autumn now. The leaves are burning.
In my dream, everything is burning.
The voices are whispering and I am burning.
What are they whispering? In my brain
there is a great confusion of voices
and I am burning and
everything is burning.

When I was a child, in the autumn I would play
in the ruined castle by my father's house.
I would creep into the ruins late at night
and listen to the whispering. It was not owls,
or wind. It was not crickets.

In our little walled garden,
the birds and animals would come
and eat right from my hand.
Papa said rather than let me go
he would drown me with his own hands.
My father had very strong hands.

Sometimes in my dream I'm drowning.
But more often I am burning,

57

and there's a whispering in my head,
voices in my head, they babble at me,
like water gurgling in a stream, or birds,
or the crackling of a fire.

This power inside me, the place
the voices come from, so
wonderful, this feeling of such
power, such control, that
nobody suspected in a young girl,
where it comes from is—
it was Saint Catharine, Saint Margaret and
Saint Michael who spoke to me.
It was not devils. Saint Catharine
communicates with me
through the spy hole in my cell,
before my execution,
whispering to me while pigeons
are cooing in the eaves.
I chose to call my voices
Saint Michael and Saint Catharine
but who they really were I cannot say.
I think my voices were older than saints.

The English call them demons,
but how can one know for sure
if it is God or demons speaking to one?
If you wear men's clothes, they call you
a witch. If you tell men they're stupid,
of course they'll kill you.
If I am a witch, which kind of witch am I?
They have called me a whore,
but that's a lie. Harlot and witch girl,
naked astraddle a flying donkey,
burned for a sorceress, for communication
with evil spirits at the fairy tree.

After my trial and execution
my friend Gilles de Rais
wrote and staged a mystery play
in my honor, a passion play.
Every play is a mystery, he said,
and every life a passion.
Gilles was a monster. Gilles was my friend.
Which kind of witch am I?
There were rumors I didn't die in the fire.
But I know I must have died because
I can feel the burning still, inside my skin,
inside me like an incubus. I wear
my flesh like clothing. What does it matter
what clothing I wear, what flesh?
These questions of identity
are bottomless, they are
a hall of mirrors.

I know that I hear voices
because my voices tell me
I hear voices.
I have a torn and ragged deck of tarot cards.
The ruined tower. The lady pope. The fool.
His face is the face of a beggar
who came to our town when I was a child.
I have a memory of burning.

My brothers say that I am Joan,
and so I must be, as I remember
dying in the fire. And they should know.
They're her brothers. And my brothers.
And her sister is dead, and so is mine,
and everything is a mystery play,
and so it must follow that this play
which is her play, is my play.

I was born on the night of Epiphany,
as the cocks began to crow. False dawn.
When I close my eyes I can feel
the stone house in Domremy all around me.
In my mind I walk in this house in the dark.

Mist under the fairy tree.
An ancient weeping beech, whispering there.
The branches hung low to the ground.
You could crawl inside and be safe
in a little cave we called the ladies' house.
A boy from the village would go there
to dance with a fairy girl at night.
And I would go at night
and lie under the fairy tree,
embraced by the gnarled roots
and branches like a lover,
and listen, and I could hear
faint moans of pleasure.

My dead sister lying among the candles.
This is the face and body of God.

I'm thirteen. It's midday, in the summertime,
in my father's garden. I hear a voice
upon the right side, towards the churchyard,
and there is a kind of brightness.

When I heard the voice three times
I knew it was an angel.
Once I beheld a multitude of angels
in the guise of certain very tiny things.
Sometimes my apparitions come
in great multitudes, and in
very tiny dimensions.
The colors are extremely pure and clear.

The voices speak in loneliness.
When there was a great clatter
and bother in the prison
I could not hear Saint Catharine.
Yet other times the voices would come
when I was desperate to concentrate
upon some other thing which I found
important at the time, and I could not
focus my attention. When my judges
held a seance so I could hear my voices
and tell them what the voices said,
I heard the voices whispering, but I
could not make out what they were saying.

What? What are you saying?
I can't hear what you're saying.
It is all a great babble of noise
and whispering and strange cries,
as if out of a great chaos, like
the lost souls in pandemonium.
Speak up or be silent, will you?
Are you trying to drive me mad?
You will make them believe that you
are demons, or that I am mad.
You make them believe I am mad.

Often I would hear the voices
when the curate rang the bell.
The sound of the bells
would draw the voices
like white butterflies.

Saint Michael told me about the war
of the angels in heaven, the war between
God and Satan, when many fell.
When Saint Michael whispers tenderly

in my ear, I can feel his warm breath
on my face, and I am strong. I'm a warrior.
Saint Michael is very handsome.

Saint Catharine is the patroness for the
prevention of fires. When I touch her
as she appears in her visible form
with the finger upon which I wear my ring,
I feel a kind of marriage
akin to her marriage with Christ.
When they burned me she must
have been in another place.

Sometimes I see faces
looking in the windows at me.
I think they're the faces of saints,
although sometimes they seem unkind,
but at other times merely sad for me.
I have called them Saint Catharine
and Saint Margaret, and I believe
them to be so. But in the dark,
lying in the dark,
I have my doubts.

Sometimes in the night I long
to touch them and be touched by them.
But I fear their touch. I fear
all touching, and yet I crave it
more than anything. For I think
that what we fear and what we want
are often the same thing. I do not know
if Saint Michael has hair or not. But once
I dreamed he touched me in a place—
but these are private matters. I don't like
old men interrogating me about these things.

Will you stop asking me these stupid questions?
I would rather you simply cut off my head.

When looked at directly,
my creatures fade.
They can only be seen
out the corner of one's eye,
only heard when one
isn't listening for them.
Those who have murdered
their own capacity
to hear voices and see visions
want to kill this precious gift in me.
If you have a gift, they will do
everything they can to murder it.

Saint Catharine embraced me and smelled of sweet
perfume, and I trembled like a lamb.
I saw them with the eyes of my body
more clearly than you can see me,
and I wept when they left me,
and prayed that they
would take me away with them,
but they would not, and yet
I believe in them as certainly
as I believe in God.

Beggars would wander into our town.
Refugees from the war. I would feed them.
A one-eyed beggar told me he also heard
voices. His voices told him that God lived
in a barn somewhere in Normandy.
I let him sleep in my bed. I slept on the floor.
When the voices began to speak to me
of driving out the English, I was frightened,

and told them I was just a girl who
couldn't ride or fight. Be a good girl,
the voices said, and God will help you.

The children of the village near us favored
the Burgundians. We were for the French.
We had bloody rock fights. These were my
first battles. They were very exciting.
The English stole our cows and burned our church.
This is how I knew they were devils.
And the voices began to speak in my father's garden
by the ruins of the church the English burned.
The light I saw by was the burning of our church.
All things begin and end in fire.

I couldn't tell my parents about the voices.
My mother said that when I was a child
my father had a dream one night that
I would go to war. And when he woke,
he was trembling and upset, and told
my mother he would rather drown me
with his own hands than allow it.
But I don't think he dreamed I'd be a soldier.
He dreamed I'd be a whore.
My father wished to strangle me
for reasons of the flesh.

When we fled from the Burgundians
I worked as a maid at an inn where they said
the women were whores, but they seemed
to be nice enough women, and better Christians
than many respectable persons of my acquaintance.
But their eyes were very sad.
Why could I not stop thinking of them?

The village idiot said I promised
to marry him, but it was a lie.
My father paid him to say it.
Virginity was my destiny.
And yet in my dreams
there was often copulation.
When I refused to marry
they decided I must be insane.
I had promised my virginity to my voices.

This ruse I did practice: tell my father,
I said to my uncle, that I must help your wife
in the birthing of her child.
And so by this white lie
did I escape my father,
And went to see Robert di Baudricourt
who had it in his power
to send me to the Dauphin.

It was December, the fields and ditches
dusted white. Captain Baudricourt
advised my uncle to give me a good spanking
and take me home. But when he saw me,
he changed his mind. The Sire di Baudricourt
was a gruff soldier, and a brave one, but
he had one weakness: he could not bring himself
to leave any relatively presentable virgin
in such a state for long. I wore a poor and worn
red dress to meet him. He looked at me the way a cat
looks at a rabbit. He was looking through my dress
at my bare flesh. His eyes devoured me.
He thought I was charmed by devils,
but sent me to the Dauphin anyway
because he liked my breasts.
I have the power to read men's minds
because there is very little in there.

I like animals better than men.
I like sheep because they are foolish.
And horses because they are not sheep.
In the eyes of sheep sometimes I see God.
In the eyes of horses I see truth.
But in the eyes of men
I see lust and violence.
What does it matter if my flesh is shaped
a certain way, or whose clothes I wear?
To put on the clothes of a man is a sin, they say.
But I can ride in a man's clothes, and fight
in a man's clothes. God doesn't care
what we wear. When God looks at us,
he sees us all naked, as he made us.
To God, we are all naked people.

Women were called to verify my virginity.
Looking between my legs and poking about,
and lighting matches so they could see better.
What did they hope to find in there? The Holy Grail?

The Duke of Alencon said my breasts are beautiful.
But I do not bleed with the moon like other women.
I think this is the mark of God, or of somebody.
When I returned from Nancy, riding a black horse,
the curate called me a thing of evil.
I was horrified. How could he know this?
And the voices came jabbering, jabbering at me.
The most serious question in the world is,
can one trust one's own voices, or can't one?
But already it was too late. I'd made my choice.

At night, I dream of the rain
on the road to Chinon,
and the dead men and animals

in the swollen river. We travel at night
and sleep in deserted houses,
or under egg yolk moons.
Often I slept between two men.
They seldom bother me.
All men are afraid of me.
As I rode across the bridge
a man made vulgar comments
about my virginity. I told him
he should be more charitable,
seeing how close he was to death.
He fell off the bridge and was drowned.
What a feeling of power this gave me.
Power is good, I thought.
The voices must have told me
he was going to fall, although
I don't remember it. I dream now
of falling in the water.

The Dauphin was ugly and treacherous.
He was God's representative on earth.
God has trouble getting good help.
I came to save him and he betrayed me.
All men are like this. Jesus must have his Judas
or there would not be thirteen at table
and the tale could not be told properly.
My life was like a fairy tale. But which one?

The Dauphin was terrified
of riding over a bridge.
He could not remain in a room
with a plank floor. He feared wood,
which is what his head was made of.
He was always afraid the floor
would collapse under him.

And one day, of course, it did.
His father, the old King, was mad as a June bug.
He'd been driven insane by tarot cards,
believed that the figures on the cards were
whispering to him in the night.
They kept hauling people out and telling me
they were the Dauphin, but I knew they weren't.
I could spot him at once because
he was the ugliest little weasel there
and because he was shuffling again and again
his father's ragged pack of cards.

The Dauphin must have a sign before
he would believe me. What sign was it?
I promised my voices I'll never tell.
If you ask me, I'll tell you a lie.
Sometimes lies are needed for God's work.
Stories and plays are necessary lies.
I told him something about himself
which none could or should know but God.
In truth, I wanted to worship him,
but this made him uneasy.
He knew his soul was weak, but he feared me.
He put me in a tower and crossed a little bridge
to see me every day, to show how brave he was.
It was where they'd locked the Templars up,
before they were tortured and burned.
There were coded messages written on the walls.
One said, I beg God to pardon me. The knight
who wrote it was burned like a potato.
At night I dreamed of two eyes in the flames.

When the learned churchmen questioned me,
I saw sheep baaing at me. Then they sent
Yolanda, the Queen of Sicily, and three other ladies
to look between my legs again. Why are men

forever wanting somebody to look between
my legs? And my impression, forgive me,
was that these three distinguished ladies
didn't know much about virginity,
but if they wanted to look between my legs,
who was I to deny them this pleasure?

The English called me a whore and made me cry.
Often I weep when I pray, as I wept
when they massacred the English prisoners.
One girl I knew at the inn would weep
each time a man made love to her.
When I pray, I feel that God
is making tender love me.
The English have always been
terrified of women. The French are
too vain to fear women. They are only
afraid of looking foolish, so of course
they always do.

The English had inserted themselves
in France like a man inserts himself
into a woman. A riddle: sixty men
and a herd of pigs creep through
the English lines and into the city
at the seige of Orleans. Who can tell
which are which?

I rode into Orleans on a white horse
at eight in the evening
during much thunder
and a great rain.
Cartloads of rotting fish are
spilled all over the battlefield
in my dream.

I was excited by the thought of battle
until I saw blood shed. Then I was still
excited but also sick with melancholy.
Sometimes the men lied to me about
their strategy, but I can always tell
when men are lying, because they talk to you
the way they talk to their dog.
Some treated me like a saint,
others a child, or a whore,
and some like the village idiot.
In short, I was treated as men
have always treated women.
In battle, men are often drowned
by the weight of their armor.
But women float.

A suit of armor is important
to cover up your body.
To go into battle naked
is a terrible thing for a virgin.
So I put on my armor. And I dreamed
of a sword hidden in the crypt of a church.
If you rub it, the rust falls off.
Swords are a form of necromancy.
I didn't like to use my sword.
It was not my purpose to kill,
although I am also good with a lance.
But I could not help going after
the prostitutes who followed the army.
Perhaps God understands death,
but I don't. I never killed a man.
But I killed a woman once.
I was chasing a prostitute
and when I whacked her
with my sword, it broke.
I'd forbidden my soldiers

to frequent prostitutes.
But why was I so angry at her?
I was consumed with passion,
and the voices were gabbling
in my head. Why am I so obsessed
with these lost women?
Something in them torments me.
I think of them lying naked
and a fire burns in my head.
Nothing was the same after
I broke my sword in that woman.
I see her in my nightmares,
the look on her face when her flesh
was pierced by my sword.
But I, too, have been wounded,
like Jesus. Once in a culvert I stepped
on a ball with spikes, like a hedgehog.
And when I was helping to raise
a ladder up to an earthwork
I was hit by the bolt of a crossbow,
just above my breast.
I wept when I saw the blood.
They put olive oil and pig's grease on it.
I went and prayed in a vineyard.
But the French were retreating,
so I took up my standard
and ran towards the enemy,
and the men rose up and followed me,
like a flock of birds in a cornfield.
Men do not generally move
unless they are chasing women.
I was probably delirious.
Delirium is helpful in religion, war, and love.
Delirium is God in your head.

In my dreams I see them

slaughtering the English prisoners.
They killed those who were not
worth ransoming. I listened
to a dying Englishman's confession.
His eyes were very blue.
There were white butterflies
all around me.

My voices had begun to quarrel.
They had doubts about my destiny.
Someone said I stole the Bishop's horse,
but that's a lie. The Bishop's horse
stole me. He was following my voices.
I went down in a ditch once
with Gilles de Rais
and he told me he also heard voices,
but his voices urged him
to murder the innocent.
I trust my voices, I said.
And I trust mine, he said.
But your voices are evil, I said.
And what are yours? he said
Many have also died for your voices.
It was true.

It was soon after this, at Paris,
that a man shot an arrow
deep into my thigh.
Deep water in the moat.
Blood in the water. My blood.
After this penetration into my flesh
I could feel my power draining away.
After Paris, darkness, a great wheel
turning downwards now,
the creaking of the windmill.
When one is penetrated, one is lost.

They have said I am a fairy girl,
but I am lost. In my dreams,
someone is kissing my naked feet.
In the woods at night,
there are strange lights.

They put me in a house to recover.
The servant girl saw me naked in the bath.
Her eyes. I shared a bed with her.
I don't like to sleep with old women.
Young girls are best. I crave the warmth.
I slept also with a woman who heard voices,
because she told me a white lady
came to her in the night.
But nobody came.

A girl had a stillborn child. They brought it to me.
I prayed. The child yawned three times and
was baptized. Then it looked at me and died.
It looked at me, and I saw the growing darkness.

Easter week Saint Catharine and Saint Margaret
began to whisper that I would be taken
before Midsummer. I was nervous
and anxious and could not rest.
When I slept with a rich man's wife,
I kept rousing her to warn her husband
about the treachery of the Burgundians.
You must always take the enemy from behind.

They'd left me two hundred Italians.
Do you know what it's like to be
a virgin among two hundred Italians?
Then one day my Italians fled, and I
was taken by Burgundians, and trapped
in an octagon. The tower of Beaurevoir.

There were ravens watching me
as I looked down from the tower,
and pigeons and doves.
Everything was very real, as if
God was hiding from me, but not far.
Distance, I thought, is an illusion.
I know that when Satan took Jesus
to a high place in the wilderness
and dared him to cast himself down,
Jesus refused. I made a different choice.
I stepped out into the air,
and into the embrace of God.
Oh, to abandon myself into the emptiness
of God's embrace was a wondrous thing.
I was like one of the angels, I could feel
my wings unfolding in the air,
the powerful flapping of my wings.
I didn't wish to die. I wished to fly.

Falling takes a long time, or seems to
except it makes little sense to speak of time
when one is falling from a great height,
for time is a distortion of the brain,
it stretches and condenses with our moods.
When asked why I leapt from the tower of Beaurevoir,
I said it was because I'd rather die
than fall into the hands of the English.
But it was something else.

I landed with a great splash
in a boggy ditch, and everything
vanished like a dream, and I was back
in my father's garden, by the broken sundial,
and then I awoke, and my head hurt,
and I saw that I was not in heaven,
and I grieved and raged and wept.

For three days then I could not eat or drink,
my soul closed up with grief.

Then a one-eyed man called me a heretic
and sold me to the English, and my good friend
the Dauphin, whom I'd made a king,
abandoned me to the Inquisition.

The first thing they did, of course,
was test me for virginity.
Even the Duke of Bedford
peeped from behind a curtain
to look between my legs.
They concluded I was a virgin,
who had injured herself by horseback riding.

They put me in another tower, feet
in leg irons, chained by the waist
to an old tree stump. Then
they built an iron cage for me
in which I could be held upright,
chained by the neck, feet and hands.
I was their darkest and most thrilling fantasy,
a helpless virgin chained in a cage.
They said I was a sorceress.
They feared my powers.
The guards tormented me. First they'd pretend
I could go free, and then they'd tell me
I was to be executed in the morning.
But I could not believe they wished to kill me.
Even the English cannot be so cruel, I thought.

The worst thing was that they
were always touching me.
A tailor came to measure me for a dress,
to put me back in women's clothes,

and rubbed his chalky fingers on my breasts.
I punched him in the nose and he fell backwards
and landed in the chamber pot.
And they would reach into my cage
and touch me in the night. In my dreams
I could feel their hands on me,
like the hands of demons.

The trial was simply an excuse to burn me.
They sent a demon to my cell to question me.
He said he was my friend, but I could see
his eyes were red like burning coals.
The learned men of the church tormented me
with questions and questions and questions,
and tried to make me utter heresy.
I could see the hate and fear in their eyes.
The Bishop sent me a carp. I took a bite
and began to vomit. The doctors tried
to bleed me, but I would not let them.

They brought me to the dungeon torture chamber
to show me the instruments of their delight.
I told them it was shameful that such men
should try and frighten a poor village girl.
They ate strawberries in a garden and
voted whether or not to torture me.

I had some hope at first. A part of me
was innocent enough to think that men
of learning, pillars of the church would
in the end behave like decent people.
But when I looked into their eyes I knew
what folly that was. They were more than happy
to cooperate in my incineration.

They put me on a scaffold by a crowd
and preached at me for hours, and said if I
did not submit I would be burned at once.
The executioner would not meet my eyes.
I thought of my poor flesh on fire.
I asked the voices what to do.
But there was silence in my head.
The voices had abandoned me.
I pitied my poor flesh.
And so I signed their foolish piece of paper.

The moment I had done so, I could hear
the voices whispering in my head again,
telling me I'd committed a betrayal
worse than Judas. And the English
were very angry, for they love bonfires.
They shaved my head. I don't know why.
In bed my legs were held by irons,
my body by a chain. The voices jabbered at me
all night long. In the morning,
the soldier stripped off my women's clothes
and I huddled naked there, begging
for something to cover my body.
They threw me back men's clothes.
I told them I was forbidden on pain of death
to put the men's clothes on again,
but they would not listen.
A great English lord tried to rape me,
but he stopped when he looked in my eyes.
I could not bear them gaping at my nakedness,
so I put on men's clothes again. This was
the sign I had denied my recantation.

I did not argue then. I knew I'd rather
burn than have them touch my flesh again.
My voices told me I would soon be free.

I could see now that they had deceived me.
They always knew that burning was my destiny.

The English put me in a cart.
I wore a black shift,
and a kerchief on my head,
and I was sobbing like a child.
The wood was piled up high
so everyone could see me burn.
There was a sign above me which said
Joan, who called herself the Maid,
a liar, pernicious deceiver of the people,
sorceress, blasphemer of God, defamer of
the faith of Jesus Christ, boastful,
idolatrous, cruel, dissolute, invoker of demons,
apostate, schismatic and heretic.

They preached a long sermon while I waited
to burn. When men are about to do something
cowardly and shameful, they give a sermon first.
The text was, "Whether one member suffer,
all the members suffer with it."
I was cast into outer darkness.
I knelt and began to pray.
The English guards were laughing at me.

Ten thousand people came to watch me burn.
A play in which the performer actually dies
is always particularly interesting to the
spectators. I was dragged to the stake.
As they chained me to the post,
I saw Saint Michael standing there among them.
I begged for a cross, and a soldier made me one
from two sticks, which I put inside my shift,
between my breasts. They tied my hands.

The fire was lit. The flames and smoke
began to envelop me. I was burning.
I cried for holy water, but there was
no water, only fire. I prayed for some
escape, but there is no escape
from the mystery one is cast in.
And after an eternity of torment,
the screaming stopped
and there was nothing.

They raked back the coals
and my naked corpse was shown
to the assembled audience, who stared
in silence at the holy mystery
of naked flesh. This was to remove
all doubt. But what can remove all doubt
but madness? Only the madness
of God can remove all doubt.

Then they burned my flesh to ashes
and threw them in the Seine.
The man who lit the fire went mad.

Now they say that I am her. And I think
I must be her, because my brothers
tell me so, and because these things
I do remember like a dream, and
because there is always burning in my head.

It's autumn now. The leaves are burning.
In my dream, everything is burning.

(The light fades on her and goes out.)

END OF PLAY

WARBURTON'S COOK

CHARACTERS

Dorry Roach, a housemaid
Betsy Baker, cook and housekeeper
John Warburton, an antiquarian

SETTING

A kitchen in the London home of John Warburton in the
early eighteenth century. A table, three chairs, and
some pies.

John Warburton (1682-1759), antiquary, an enthusiastic
collector who owned many valuable and rare manuscripts.
Most of these—many the only extant copies of Elizabethan
and Jacobean plays—were, through his own "carelessness, and
the ignorance" of Betsy Baker, his servant, "unluckily burned
or put under pye bottoms."

"Sin in a ditch. Double bubble, drabble scrabble, Judith's house
will be a Wimpy's, Warburton's cook will bake you in a nice
meat pie. Take, eat."
                    —the Fool in *Loves Labours Wonne.*

WARBURTON'S COOK

(The kitchen of the house of JOHN WARBURTON the anti-quarian. Early 18th century. BETSY BAKER, Warburton's housekeeper, is baking pies. DORRY ROACH, the house-maid, is sitting at a wooden table, eating pie.)

DORRY. Oh, Betsy, this is such fine pie. It's almost better than kissing.

BETSY. Pie is the secret of life. If you want to know how to make a man happy, Dorry Roach, learn how to bake pies. It isn't just the pleasure he gets eating your pies that will en-slave his soul to you, but also the anticipation, and the smell of pies baking. The smell creeps through the house and finds him wherever he is, and is a way of touching him. He knows you're there. He sniffs you up his nostrils. The smell of bak-ing pie goes anyplace he is, he can't escape it. Soon the pie is all he can think about, and you are the maker of pies. The smell draws him to you, and he loves you for it.

DORRY. And you think Master Warburton loves you, Betsy?

BETSY. He loves my pies. It's more or less the same thing. He loves my apple pies, he loves my cherry pies, he loves my berry pies, he loves my meat pies. I can't get the man to look in my eyes, but he'll look at my pies, stare into my pies with love in his eyes. So I bake him pies.

DORRY. I think it's an odd circumstance that such a great man as Master Warburton should love pies so.

BETSY. Pies is what makes us all one, Dorry. Pies is the great leveller. Get a man habituated to enjoying your pies, and he'll be your slave forever. Great or small, gentleman or dung-shoveller, pies is the secret vice of them all. Pies is the secret of life.

DORRY. I think Master Warburton must be a very great man indeed, as he has so many books and papers, he can hardly move about in his study.

BETSY. Oh, he's a wondrous cluttered man, is Master Warburton. So much rubbish he's got laying about. He's a lovely man but he's got a mind like a rabbit dance. All this crumbly old paper rubbish somebody's great grandfather has scribbled and dripped all over. What a mess.

DORRY. And he won't let me clean in there, neither.

BETSY. The trick is to sneak in when he's at the coffee house, which is what I do, to try and redd up as best as I can. For such a wise man, and so learned, with so many books, his head stuffed with so many cobwebbed particularities, he's a very foolish, distracted and disorderly man. But I creep in and redd up when he's not there, and he never knows the difference.

DORRY. But what if he should come back unexpected and surprise you?

BETSY. We must run some risks for those we love, Dorry. Love is a dangerous thing. But I'm proud to say, I've always had the courage to look after him no matter what. I nursed him when he was sick, when the housemaid that was before you ran away, for fear she'd catch the fever. And he takes no care of his health. He never thinks about the fire at all, so wrapped up is he in his work. If I did not keep it burning night and day, the poor man would freeze to death. They'd find him sitting there at his desk, surrounded by books and clutter, frozen like the pump, with icicles hanging off him, if it weren't for me keeping up the fire.

DORRY. Do you never think to marry, Betsy, and get away from here? You're still a young woman, and Bob the Footman's sweet on you.

BETSY. You can have Bob the Footman. It is my great pleasure to keep Master John Warburton warm and full of pie.

DORRY. But do you never get lonely at night in bed?

BETSY. I'm too busy thinking of him to be lonely. What I will bake tomorrow. If he has gone to sleep yet. I always sit up when he works late in his study, in case he needs anything. He tells me to go to bed, but I won't, for if it didn't play upon his guilt for preventing my rest, he'd sit up over his books and papers till the cock crows.

DORRY. I think you are sick in love with the man, Betsy.

BETSY. Love is in the doing, Dorry. I love him with fire and pies.

DORRY. What do you suppose he's always reading and writing about?

BETSY. He's an antiquarian, which means, as near as I can gather, that he studies what nobody else has cared about in a hundred years, and roots around in the papers of dead people, looking for what, I don't know. I'd never want to learn to read, myself. I think it's a dangerous habit. It only distracts one from getting done the important things, like feeding the fire and baking pies.

WARBURTON. *(Shouting from off.)* Dorry.

BETSY. And there is the voice of the great man himself, with a burr up his arse about something.

DORRY. Yes, sir?

WARBURTON. Have you been messing about in my study?

DORRY. What, sir?

WARBURTON. *(Appearing in the kitchen.)* Have you been moving things about in my study?

DORRY. No, sir.

WARBURTON. I told you to stay out of there.

DORRY. I haven't been in there, sir.

WARBURTON. Well, somebody has.

DORRY. Perhaps it's the rats, sir.

WARBURTON. It's not the rats. I can't find a number of manuscripts I know were there not long ago.

BETSY. I wonder you can find anything in there. It's a miracle you don't lose track of your own backside in all that clutter.

WARBURTON. Dorry, if you've been in my study, you must tell me now.

BETSY. She hasn't been in your study.

WARBURTON. Then who has?

BETSY. I've been in there a time or two. Would you like a piece of pie?

WARBURTON. No, I don't want a damned piece of pie, woman, I want to know where my manuscripts are. What have you done with my manuscripts?

BETSY. Your manuskips? I've seen no manuskips. I'm sure I wouldn't know a manuskip if it skipped up and bit me. Look at these pies.

WARBURTON. Manuscripts.

BETSY. I don't know nothing about anything like that, but I'm not surprised you can't locate them, with all those old scribbled-on pieces of paper stacked about in there.

WARBURTON. Betsy, listen to me. I had stored in my study fifty-five rare and irreplaceable Elizabethan and Jacobean manuscripts. Playscripts. Handwritten copies of plays written in the Elizabethan and Jacobean period. Some were nearly a hundred and fifty years old.

BETSY. Yes, well, they looked like it. All spotted and blotched with mildew. It isn't healthy to sit in the midst of all that rubbish all day. It's a haven for lice and rats and God knows what else. If I was you, sir, I wouldn't fret over a bunch of smelly old plays. Just sit down and have a piece of pie and say good riddance to them.

WARBURTON. Betsy, what have you done?

BETSY. I've done what I've always done. I've made you some nice meat pies, and cherry pies.

WARBURTON. You haven't thrown them out, have you? Oh, God, Betsy, tell me you haven't thrown them out.

BETSY. No, I haven't thrown them out. They're right here cooling on the table.

WARBURTON. Not the pies, you imbecile. The manuscripts. Have you thrown out my manuscripts?

BETSY. I am not an imbecile. I am a decent Christian woman, and I haven't thrown out your precious rubbish.

WARBURTON. Thank God. Where are they?

BETSY. I've been using them to get the fire going. They burn very nicely. And the rest I've used to line pie bottoms.

WARBURTON. You've been lighting the fire with my manuscripts?

BETSY. And lining the pie bottoms. So you can rest easy that nothing's gone to waste.

WARBURTON. Jesus Christ.

BETSY. Here, now, sir. Unless you are commencing to lead us in prayer, there's no call to bring Jesus into this matter.

WARBURTON. Do you know what you've done? Do you have any idea what you've done?

BETSY. I've baked you some lovely pies, is what I've done. You know you love my pies.

WARBURTON. I don't give a tinker's fart about your goddamned pies, you stupid girl. You've taken my precious, precious manuscripts and destroyed them. You've destroyed them. To light the fire. To make your wretched pies.

BETSY. My pies are not wretched, sir, and you know it. I make the best pies in all of England.

WARBURTON. Will you stop yammering about pies? This is not about pies.

BETSY. Then what is it about?

WARBURTON. Among those fifty-five manuscripts, which you have used to light the fire and line pie bottoms, there were, along with other very precious and immensely rare Elizabethan and Jacobean manuscripts, there were several plays in manuscript, hitherto unpublished, virtually unknown until I came across them in the bookseller's trunk, manuscripts dating from the fifteen-nineties, manuscripts of plays attributed to, and very likely written by, William Shakespeare.

BETSY. Well, if you need them for something, just go get some more.

WARBURTON. There aren't any more.

BETSY. Of course there are more. They're putting on Shakespeare at Drury Lane all the time. You're always going there. Just get them the same place they do. And why do you need those dirty old papers anyway, when you can go and see him on the stage, with actors and such, any time you want to?

WARBURTON. These plays are not done on the stage.

BETSY. Then they can't be very good, can they?

WARBURTON. These plays were lost. I found them. These were the only copies. They are lost plays by William Shakespeare.

BETSY. Well, if he lost them, it's his own fault, isn't it?

WARBURTON. It isn't his fault, it's your fault, for going into my study when I told you to stay out of there—

BETSY. You didn't tell me to stay out of there. You told Dorry to stay out of there. And she did, didn't you, Dorry?

DORRY. I never went in there in my life. I peeked in once or twice.

WARBURTON. Oh, God. Oh, God. They're all burned. All burned. *King Henry the First. King Henry the Second. The Tragedy of Duke Humphrey. The History of King Stephen, Loves Labours Wonne, Iphis and Iantha.*

BETSY. Who?

WARBURTON. *Iphis and Iantha, or a Marriage Without A Man, a Comedy by William Shakespeare.*

BETSY. A marriage without a man? What kind of perverse thing would that be? It sounds like a stuffy, boring lot of rubbish to me, except for that last one, which I expect wasn't fit for decent people to see in the first place.

WARBURTON. Do you have no understanding of what you've done? Are you really so incredibly self-centered and utterly imbecilic that you haven't the slightest comprehension of what you've done?

BETSY. I understand what I've done. I've kept you warm when you were cold. I've nursed you when you were sick and nobody else would come near you, and I burned papers to keep you warm. And I've fed you these pies, which are worthy and good things I have made.

WARBURTON. I'm not talking about pies. I'm talking about great works of art.

BETSY. My pies is works of art to me. I made them, didn't I? I made them as much as that old gasbag Shakespeare made his stupid plays, didn't I? At least you can eat my pies. What the hell can you do with what he made, but sit and waste your time and get sore buttocks? You'd have froze to death if I hadn't burned something to keep the fire going. I nursed you back to health with soup cooked in a kettle atop a fire made of those old papers, and I lined pie bottoms with them so I could make you the meat pies that kept you alive.

WARBURTON. Pie bottoms. Pie bottoms.

(WARBURTON takes a pie and begins frantically scooping out the crust and contents.)

BETSY. Here, what are you doing to that pie? I just made that. It's hot.

WARBURTON. Owwww.

BETSY. You've burned your fingers. What are you doing to my beautiful pie? Have you gone mad?

WARBURTON. *(Pulling out strips of something like old manuscript.)* Here it is. Here it is. It's all smeared. Utterly illegible. Destroyed. All destroyed.

(WARBURTON sits down and holds his head in his hands.)

BETSY. Now you're getting pie all over your face. You're like a child. Here, let me wipe it off.

WARBURTON. Don't touch me, you cretin.

BETSY. *(Taken aback by the violence in his voice.)* All right. I won't touch you then. You didn't call me such names when I held your hand when you were nearly dead in your bed, so weak you couldn't move. You held my hand and looked at me for hours, like a child, and I stayed with you until you slept, singing you songs and telling you foolish stories to make you laugh. I know I'm just a servant. I have no illusions about my position here. But I don't deserve such treatment. And look what you've done to my beautiful pie.

(BETSY begins to cry, softly and with great dignity. WARBURTON looks at her. A long moment while she cries and he watches her. Then:)

WARBURTON. Dorry, get me some milk, and a bowl, would you?

DORRY. Yes, sir.

WARBURTON. I find I've a notion to have this pie broken up in a bowl with milk. *(DORRY gives him the bowl, puts the milk down.)* Thank you. And a spoon, please. *(He scoops up the pieces of the pie he's destroyed and puts them in the bowl. DORRY gets the spoon.)* Cherry. My favorite. Are they from Mrs Rumpley's garden?

(BETSY doesn't answer. WARBURTON pours the milk on the pie.)

DORRY. They are. Betsy got up early this morning to pick them herself. So you would have the cherry pie for when you took your break from your work. To keep your strength up. She knew you had a weakness for Mrs Rumpley's cherries.

WARBURTON. *(Eating the pie and milk.)* Oh, this is wonderful. Betsy, you've outdone yourself. This is the most extraordinary pie. It's the finest pie I've ever had in my life.

BETSY. Do you think so, sir?

WARBURTON. Oh, yes. I am very happy with this pie, Betsy. It's a work of art.

(BETSY smiles. WARBURTON eats the pie. Fade to darkness.)

END OF PLAY

HIGGS FIELD

HIGGS FIELD

*(Sound of ticking clocks in the darkness. Lights up on AN-
DROMEDA, a young girl, who speaks to the audience from
a circle of light, surrounded by darkness.)*

ANDROMEDA. Early one morning she wakes from a
dream about ravens, creeps naked from her bed, puts on her
dress, crawls out the window, makes her way down the sloped
roof, clambers down the rainspout, and runs down the shaded
path towards Higgs Field, a place she has been forbidden to
go, to search for Mrs Schroedinger's cat. The field is supposed to be haunted, an ancient burial ground of some sort.
There is a great brick wall at one end of the field, and a large
black hole at the center, like dark, bubbling quicksand. Her
friend Marie wandered into Higgs Field one night and never
returned. There is a honeycomb in a gigantic, twisted old oak
tree near the far end of the field, by Mr Gott's house. She can
hear the humming of the bees. The girl's name is Andromeda.
There is dark matter there, says the old gypsy woman, laying
out dog-eared tarot cards while her dark-eyed daughter does
not touch my breasts.
  Uncertainty rules in this place. She can see Oort's windmill
turning in the distance. Her friend Berenice is in a coma because of what she saw in this place. All her teeth have fallen
out. I go to visit her in the madhouse when it rains. Her father
was eaten by dachshunds. Across the field is the old stone house
where the Quarks live. They are a German family who survive

93

by selling curds. They are known for talking nonsense. There is a labyrinth made of hedges and brick, wood and stone, in their back garden. There are six members of the Quark family, but four of them are seldom seen. When Mrs Quark is very happy, Mr Quark is very sad.

In my youth, I went to Copenhagen, said Mrs Quark to Andromeda one day. It was a place full of windmills and sundials. I was very beautiful then. My hair would blow in the wind like the trailing branches of the weeping willow. Young men would follow me about like little dachshunds, desperate to smell my hair. That is where I met Mr Quark, on a carousel horse in the morning.

Was Mr Quark unhappy then, too? asked Andromeda.

Oh, yes, said Mrs Quark. That's what I found so attractive about him. That, and his rather large tallywhacker.

Whenever she walked through Higgs Field, she felt an overwhelming sense of strangeness, as if it were the place where gargoyles go to die. It seemed to Andromeda that Higgs Field was full of entities who were millions of times older than anyone could imagine, some made of stone, others of bread. Some of them were gargoyles, but others were once melancholy young women who walked late at night in Rose Alley, whispering sonnets and obscenities at the moon and kissing Shakespeare on the mouth. Once, in the middle of the field, she came upon a snake eating its tail. The snake had blue eyes, and it looked at her. Often small animals looked at her, and this made her tremble. They seemed to want to tell her something from a past life.

Near Higgs Field was an old house once owned by a man named Maxwell, who died of thirst and loneliness at forty-eight. A demon lives in that house now, said Mrs Quark. It was the demon who killed Mr Maxwell. The demon of loneliness often kills the good, she said. At night, Andromeda could see strange lights in the abandoned house, and something like ball lightning seemed to move about from room to room, going up and down the stairs.

There was something in Higgs Field at night. You couldn't
see it, exactly, although sometimes you could, or almost could,
but it was there. The fireflies hovering over the field on summer nights looked like stars. And the sweetness of the wild-
flowers was an ocean of fragrance in the spring. At night you
could hear voices whispering in the field, and shreds of music, Bach and Chopin played simultaneously, and sometimes
backwards. In her dreams it seemed to Andromeda that all of
time was happening at once, all ghosts past and future living
there together in the voices in the wind at night in Higgs Field.

Nearby was Isaac's apple orchard. Many years ago, old
Isaac was struck by lightning while standing under one of his
apple trees, and, forever after, all the clocks in his house said
different times. When he would walk by, the hands of the clocks
would whirl about madly backwards and forwards, as would
her grandfather's watch, which she kept on a chain between
her breasts, like a third nipple, and the cuckoos went in and
out singing at odd times. There were many books in his house
by a man named Swedenborg who had once seen God playing
at dice with Moll Flanders.

At night she would dream of Higgs Field. She dreamed she
would go there to meet her demon lover, the demon who had
killed poor Mr Maxwell. In her dream, the demon was a tall,
brooding creature with dark, sad eyes. She would redeem the
demon through her love, she thought. But when the demon
entered her, she was cold, and she shivered and shivered, and
then she woke up sobbing and drenched with sweat. For the
demon of loneliness is not a gentleman.

There were ravens in Higgs Field. They sat on the dead
trees and mourned. When she walked there in the evening,
she could smell the rotting apples. She knew that somehow
this place was an intimate part of her destiny. At the far end of
the field grazed the Higgs bison, animals which disappeared
whenever they turned sideways, like her Aunt Nell. We were
dining upon a bowl of Mrs Quark's infamous soup when she
revealed to me her great secret. Round things were floating in

the soup. They looked like sheep eyes. Andromeda, she said, the secret of God is that the past is never gone, no matter how much we may grieve for it. We are living in the past every second of our lives. The past is precisely and entirely what we are made of.

At one end of Higgs Field is the graveyard of the dwarfs. The trees here are ancient and dying, and there are fallen leaves everywhere. By the wall of the graveyard for dwarfs there are bubbles coming out of the stones. Lichen. Moss. Regret. Some of the most ancient trees have been cut down. The huge stumps are scattered through the ruined graveyard. There is fog in the morning hanging over the graveyard of dwarfs at the edge of Higgs Field. Mrs Quark collects string. She has complex webs of string hanging all over her mansion. The string is covered with cobwebs, and so is Mr Quark. Now and then he clucks like a chicken, to let her know he isn't dead.

I know from the fragments of photographs she's torn out of her scrapbooks that something terrible happened in Copenhagen in the year 1921. Someone was murdered, I think, at a haunted inn. I have come to believe, if believe is the right word, and it certainly is not the right word, but for want of a better, I have come to believe there is not one past, but many pasts. It is the tree of life with many intersecting branches. Fog over the Heisenberg woods, where one always gets lost. Sheep wander there and never return. Now and then you can hear their forlorn baas.

(Sound of forlorn sheep baaaing.)

Looking through a dark pane of glass in the ruins of the ancient chapel by Higgs Field, Andromeda becomes so melancholy, she feels an overwhelming compulsion to have a bath. There is an old photograph on the wall, of a small child with a large balloon tied around her wrist. In Mr Maxwell's abandoned house there is a statue of a naked woman with the string of a balloon tied to each of her nipples. Everything here means something but nobody knows what.

In the garden of the Quarks is an ancient crab apple tree. On the wall of the outhouse is a painting of the war of the clowns against the mimes. The clowns have horns. The mimes fight with invisible instruments. The round wooden hole leaves a red mark on Andromeda's shapely young buttocks when she pees there. She turns the pages of an ancient Burpee seed catalogue. I am the hyacinth girl, she thinks, listening to her pee splatter far below.

Baaa, say the melancholy sheep.

Would you like some more soup? asks Mrs Quark.

Mr Quark clucks softly in the corner, reading last year's newspaper under his cobwebs.

Chaos conceals design, but design fails to conceal chaos. All patterns emerge from chaos, but chaos itself is just a larger pattern, like a carpet made by a blind man. There is disorder all around us, said old Mr Hubble, peering into his magical spyglass. Andromeda looked in the spy glass one day and saw a great bloodshot eye looking back at her. Who is that? she asked. That is either God, said Mr Hubble, touching her ass reverently, or some insect on the other end of the spyglass. Often Mr Hubble uses his spyglass to peek at the house of Miss Mobius across the way. Miss Mobius is training to be a metaphysical ecdysiast. She is always taking off some clothing while putting on other clothing, so that while she is never completely revealed, she is also never completely concealed. Andromeda is taking revelation lessons from her to help prepare herself for the nudity required when she is chained to her rock by the ocean.

Hawks circle above Higgs Field. When she gets very depressed, Andromeda goes to visit the shop of Mr Gott, the blind watchmaker. Nobody is in the belltower, but the bell rings now and then. It is the ghost of a dead Scotsman. Mr Gott's house is full of worm holes and ticking clocks. All the clocks say different times. There is a sundial in the shade by the ferns. She goes into the shop and stumbles over something in the gloom. She lights a lamp and sees that she has stepped on Mr Gott, whose corpse is decomposing there among the ticking clocks. He smells like rotting apples. Oh, no, she thinks. Now that Mr Gott is dead, the clocks will chime and die, one by one, chime and die. Who will wind the clocks now? She runs about the shop, frantically winding clocks, stepping gingerly over the corpse as she goes back and forth. The ravens have eaten his eyes. Soon I must go and be chained to my rock, and there will be nobody to wind up the clocks again forever. Tick. Tock. Tick. Tock. Tick. And then they stop.

A memory. Andromeda has a sudden memory, which blows through her head like wind after rain. I am a small child sitting at a kitchen table in Munich, Germany a hundred years ago, and a strange man is reading a book about clocks to me. It's a dream. I know it's a dream. And yet I am lost. Andromeda is lost. In Higgs Field, the ravens are waiting to feast on my brain.

Andromeda sits sobbing in the rain, all among the broken clocks, when Mrs Schroedinger's cat appears from under the piano, settles itself on her lap and purrs and purrs and purrs. She pets the cat and kisses its head. Something is moving slowing towards her in the rain across Higgs Field. Something is moving towards her.

(The light fades on her and goes out.)

END OF PLAY

THINGS THAT GO BUMP IN THE NIGHT

CHARACTERS

Ben
Tracy

SETTING

A living room, late at night.
A sofa. A table with a lamp.

THINGS THAT GO BUMP IN THE NIGHT

(Night. Sound of ticking clocks in the darkness. TRACY sits in the dark, wearing pajama tops. BEN enters, wearing the bottoms, turns on the light.)

TRACY. Turn that light off.

BEN. What is it now?

TRACY. Just turn it off.

BEN. Why?

TRACY. Because I'm sitting in the dark.

BEN. Why are you sitting in the dark?

TRACY. I'm waiting.

BEN. Waiting for what?

TRACY. None of your business.

BEN. What are you waiting for in our living room at four o'clock in the morning? A streetcar?

TRACY. If I tell you, you'll make fun of me.

BEN. I won't make fun of you.

TRACY. You always make fun of me.

BEN. Sometimes I have no choice.

TRACY. You'll think I'm insane.

BEN. I already think you're insane.

TRACY. All right. You remember that production of *Betrayal* we saw?

BEN. What about it?

TRACY. You remember all the futons?

BEN. Futons?

TRACY. You know. Those big stuffed things you put on the floor, with no legs, like gigantic pillow couches and chairs and stuff, like giant egg plant sections you can move around and stack on top of each other to make these big floppy soft furniture things? Futons.

BEN. You're sitting here in the dark at four in the morning thinking about futons? You think we should get rid of the furniture and buy futons? This is what's troubling you?

TRACY. I am not troubled by futons. I hate futons.

BEN. Then why are we talking about them?

TRACY. Because you asked me what was bothering me.

BEN. You said futons weren't bothering you.

TRACY. I can't talk to you.

BEN. Is it something about the play? Is Pinter bothering you? Are you thinking about betraying me with Harold Pinter?

TRACY. Do you want to hear this or what?

BEN. More than life itself.

TRACY. This production of *Betrayal* we saw, the one with all the futons, if you'll remember, it was a pretty good production, in most respects, right? I mean, the play is good, and the actors were good, the scenes were played well, but their production concept was, they had all these futons, right?

BEN. Right.

TRACY. And when each scene was over, the lights would go out, and these people dressed in black clothes with black ski masks would scuttle out in the dark and move the futons into different positions, so that when the lights came up, we were supposed to understand that we were in a different place, right? Their concept was to move these futons around between each scene and stack them up in different ways to create futon couches and futon beds and things from various different arrangements of these big-ass futons, right?

BEN. But this is not about futons.

TRACY. No. This is not about futons.

BEN. Then what is this about?

TRACY. Well, as the play went on, I'd get caught up in the scenes, in the play itself, which is a great play, but when the scene was over, you could see these people dressed all in black, like cat burglars sneaking on in the dark and moving these futons all over the place like there's no tomorrow, you know?

BEN. Yes?

TRACY. And it seemed like each scene change took longer than the one before it, so that after a while, they were taking almost as long to rearrange the futons as the scenes took before and after all this futon moving.

BEN. And the recollection of this leads you to sit out here in the dark at four o'clock in the morning because—?

TRACY. So three quarters of the way through the play, we're in the dark more than we're in the light, and the black futon movers are getting more time onstage than the actors, and the play itself seems to be less and less important, and the futon moving more and more important, until by the end, these people in black are taking so much time moving the futons around in the dark with such maniacal frenzy that it's no longer a play about betrayal at all, it's a play about these weird little people dressed in black moving these goddamned futons.

BEN. And that's why you can't sleep?

TRACY. I can't sleep because I can't stop thinking about it.

BEN. About futons?

TRACY. No.

BEN. About shit-headed directors who come up with grotesquely stupid production concepts that lengthen the playing time by a half hour and totally muck up a perfectly good play?

TRACY. No, about those people dressed in black.

BEN. The futon movers?

TRACY. Yes.

BEN. What about them?

TRACY. Did you ever notice that when we get up in the morning, the furniture seems to be in slightly different places?

BEN. No, I never did.

TRACY. Well, you should pay more attention to things like that. You nearly broke your neck the other night falling over the antimacassar.

BEN. I didn't fall over the antimacassar.

TRACY. You did too, you big liar.

BEN. You can't fall over an antimacassar.

TRACY. You can.

BEN. An antimacassar is something old ladies drape over the back of a chair to keep from getting hair oil on it.

TRACY. Then what did you fall over?

BEN. I fell over the footstool.

TRACY. It's not a footstool. It's an ottomacassar.

BEN. Ottoman.

TRACY. Okay, something Turkish. I don't care. The point is, you fell over it because it was in a different place in the middle of the night than it was when we went to bed.

BEN. No it wasn't.

TRACY. Then why did you fall over it?

BEN. Because I didn't see it.

TRACY. But why didn't you see it?

BEN. Because it was dark.

TRACY. Exactly.

BEN. Exactly what?

TRACY. That's when they move things around. In the dark.

BEN. Who does?

TRACY. The people who move things around at night.

BEN. What people?

TRACY. The futon people.

BEN. Have you been putting gin in your Dr. Pepper again?

TRACY. Well, it's good that way.

BEN. You don't think there's futon people out here running around in our living room in the dark while we're sleeping, do you?

TRACY. There could be.

BEN. No there couldn't.

TRACY. Why couldn't there?

BEN. For one thing, we don't have any futons.

TRACY. They don't just move futons. They move all kinds of furniture.

BEN. How the hell do you know?

TRACY. Because I've seen them in other productions.

BEN. This is not a production. This is our life.

TRACY. But I've been hearing things.

BEN. Of course you've been hearing things. You put gin in your Dr. Pepper. It's a wonder you've got any brain cells left.

TRACY. At night, when you're asleep, sometimes I just lie there, kind of half asleep and half awake, in that sort of weird in-between state where all these strange images and things float up into your head, and I can hear things, in other parts of the house, even sometimes in our bedroom. I hear things.

BEN. We've got mice.

TRACY. Mice can't move the furniture.

BEN. Nobody's been moving the furniture.

TRACY. I think somebody is. And I just wonder if maybe it isn't somebody like those futon people dressed in black coming into our house at night and rearranging the furniture.

BEN. Tracy, trust me, really, the furniture is always in the exact same place in the morning as it was when we went to bed at night.

TRACY. Is it?

BEN. Of course it is.

TRACY. Then why do you keep falling over it? You're like Dick Van Dyke out here.

BEN. I fall over the furniture because I'm clumsy. I'm near-sighted and absent minded and I can't see in the dark and sometimes I come out here to go to the bathroom in the middle of the night and I fall over something, but that doesn't mean there are phantom futon people rearranging the furniture while we're sleeping.

TRACY. Have you been keeping careful track of where all the furniture is?

BEN. Yes. I have a chart. I check it every night before I go to sleep, and in the morning, it's always the way I left it.

TRACY. Well, but maybe they move it back.

BEN. They move it back?

TRACY. Well, obviously.

BEN. They wait until we're asleep, then they sneak out here and rearrange the furniture, and then they move it all back before morning.

TRACY. It's a theory.

BEN. Why the hell would they want to do that?

TRACY. I don't know. Why the hell did they do it in the Pinter play? The futons were perfectly fine where they were. They could have just left them there and played right from one scene to the next without any breaks at all, and the play would have taken a good forty-five minutes less, and my butt would have gotten a lot less sore, and I could have peed forty-five minutes sooner, but no, the goddamned futon people had to keep coming out and interrupting, they had to keep meddling, they had to keep tinkering, because that's what they do. They're insidious. Demonic. It's absolutely terrifying, when you think about it.

BEN. It certainly is.

TRACY. I'm not talking to you any more, ever again.

BEN. All right. Let's presume these mysterious people dressed in black appear in our house after we go to bed and move our furniture around all night in the dark and then put it back where it was, or almost where it was, and then disappear back into the cupboards like the Clabber Girl and the Little Dutch Boy in the old cartoon. What's the difference? What harm do they do? It's like trying to convince somebody there's a parallel universe to ours that's exactly the same in almost every way, but we can never go there or know anything about it. So what?

TRACY. But their universe crosses ours. They invade ours.

BEN. And that means we should do what?

TRACY. Well, I have a plan.

BEN. I was afraid you might.

TRACY. We could stay up and listen for them.

BEN. Yes? And then what?

TRACY. Maybe we could catch them in the act.

BEN. And then what?

TRACY. Then we'd know.

BEN. We'd know that you're insane, and I'm insane for getting up in the middle of the night to chase around imaginary people dressed in black who spend all night rotating my antimacassars. *(Pause.)* Tracy?

TRACY. You really do think I'm insane, don't you? You're not joking. You think I'm certifiable. Some day you're going to have me committed so you can take all my money, aren't you?

BEN. You don't have any money.

(Pause.)

TRACY. Would you ever betray me?

BEN. No. I would never betray you.

TRACY. Why?

BEN. Because I love you.

TRACY. Uh huh.

(Pause.)

BEN. So maybe it's a play. Our life. Maybe it's a play, and we're cast in the play, and when we sleep, it's intermission and these backstage people need to come out and do whatever it is they do, for whatever reasons, rearrange the futons, whatever. And maybe in this particular play the woman I love is— has a unique imagination. And a lot of deep insecurities. And maybe she just sees more deeply into the nature of things than I do, than other allegedly normal people do. That's what makes it a good play. No matter how stupid the director is, or how dumb the transitions are. This is our play. Yours and mine. And I'm not leaving until the end. Because I want to see what happens. Because you're a wonderful character. And it's a privilege and an adventure to work with you. So you don't ever, ever have to lose any sleep over that, okay? Tracy? *(Pause.)* Move over.

TRACY. Why?

BEN. *(Sitting down beside her, and pulling her over onto his lap.)* We're going to turn out the light, and wait for those futon people to show up.

TRACY. But what if they never come out when you're watching?

BEN. Then I won't fall over the antimacassar.

(BEN kisses TRACY very tenderly. She puts her head on his shoulder. He turns out the light. Darkness.)

END OF PLAY

UNCLE CLETE'S TOAD

UNCLE CLETE'S TOAD

(UNCLE CLETE, an old man, speaks to the audience from his kitchen table in the morning, drinking his coffee. The year is perhaps 1962.)

UNCLE CLETE. So I hear this loud shriek, and a whole mess of little yappy barking in the morning as I'm just sitting down for a cup of coffee with my parakeet Wendell Willkie, and Molly comes into the kitchen and says Cletis, there's a big toad weighing himself on the bathroom scale.

—How much does he weigh? I ask her. She didn't think it was funny. She hasn't laughed at anything I've said in about thirty-five years, unless I was serious, of course. I become amorous late at night, she thinks that's hysterical.

—Molly, you've got to stop drinking that Jim Beam in the morning, I say to her.

—Get your sorry old ass in there and get rid of that toad, she says. It's upsetting the Little Old Man.

The Little Old Man is our toy poodle. He's got less brain than a doughnut and he's terrified of cockroaches, and is a very silly little person altogether, but we love him, so I let Wendell nibble at my toast while I get up and go around the corner to the bathroom, and I stumble over the Little Old Man, who's running around in little hysterical circles yapping, and I throw him out into the kitchen and close the door, and then I have to bend down with my hands on my knees to get a proper

111

look, as I can't see worth shit any more, and sure enough, squatting there on the bathroom scale is this big old fat toad, just as happy as you please, like the King of France sitting on his throne.

—Don't you hurt it, says Molly, from the other side of the door. Just get it out of here.

So I go and get my gloves and a bucket from the garage, and then I come back in and pick up the toad, put him in the bucket, take him out to the back yard and let him loose under the apple tree.

—Goodbye, toad, I say. And I figure that's the end of it.

Well, next morning, I'm just sitting down to my coffee and toast with Wendell Willkie when I hear this same loud shriek again and the yapping and carrying on, and Molly comes into the kitchen and says, I thought I told you to get rid of that toad, and I says I got rid of the toad, you saw me get rid of the toad. And she says, well, he's back.

So I leave my toast to Wendell again and get up and go around the corner and trip over the damned dog again and throw him out and close the door and bend down and look and damn if that toad isn't right back there sitting on that bathroom scale.

— Well, I said. How the hell are you getting in here, Mr Toad? Because I sealed up every corner in this place last year when we had the rats under the house. I know there's no place in this room anywhere near big enough for a big old toad like you to get in here. So where the hell did you come from? But the toad just sits there. I guess I didn't really expect any answers.

—Don't hold a conversation with him, just get rid of it, says Molly, from the other side of the door. I've got to pee. But don't you hurt him.

So I go out to the garage again and get my gloves and the bucket, and this time I take the toad across the alley to the field back there by the hill and let him loose in the weeds, and then I go back in the house and sit down and watch Wendell pecking at my toast and I say, Wendell, I wonder how that damned toad got in here? I just don't see how he could. And Wendell he just cocks one eye up at me like he does, and he says, You're a dirty bird.

—I know it, Wendell, I says.

So the next morning, I'm sitting down with my coffee and toast at the kitchen table and there comes that shriek and the yapping again, and here comes Molly around the corner, and she says that damned toad is back on the bathroom scale again.

—Cletis, she says, have you been putting that toad on the bathroom scale just to irritate me in the morning? Because if this is one of your stupid practical jokes, you're going to pay for it, I swear.

—Yes, Molly, I says, I get up at six o'clock in the morning, go outside and find a toad, then come back in here and sit him on the bathroom scale just so I can hear the damned dog yapping while I'm trying to drink my coffee. That's what I do to amuse myself.

—Well, if you're not putting him in there, then how's he getting there? I thought you sealed everything up tight when we got rid of the rats.

—I did seal everything up tight, I says.

—Then where the hell is that toad coming from? she says.

—If I knew that, don't you think I'd seal it up? I says.

—I thought you sealed up everything already, she says.

—You're a dirty bird, says Wendell.

—Can't I just sit here and eat my toast in peace for one morning? I says.

—Not until you go and get rid of that toad, she says, because I've got to pee, and I'm not going to sit there and pee with a toad squatting on the bathroom scale looking at me.

—Molly, I says, that toad don't want to see you pee. He don't care about that. He's a toad.

—Just get him the hell out of there, says Molly.

Well, I knew that tone. That tone was a clear announcement that the discussion period had concluded. So I got up and left my toast to Wendell and got the gloves and the bucket and I put that toad in the bucket and I headed on out the door.

—Don't you hurt him, says Molly.

So I walked about a half mile up the hill and down the other side and over to the creek, and I let that toad out of the bucket, and I walked all the way home, and when I got back to the house, my coffee was gone, and the toast was gone, and Wendell was back in his cage, and the dog was asleep on my chair, and I was so tired I went back to bed, and the next morning I got up early to go to the bathroom, and there was that damned toad, sitting on the scale again, just as happy as a pig in shit.

Well, now, this got me to thinking, maybe it's not the same toad. Maybe we just got a very large toad population in this house, and they all look more or less the same, being related to each other, toad cousins and toad uncles and such. So before I put the toad in the bucket, I got some of Molly's lipstick, and I put a spot on his back, to mark him. Then I put him in the bucket, and put the bucket in the Buick, and drove all the way out of town towards Mad Anthony, and I put that toad by a little stream not far from the lane that used to lead to the Crab Apple Whorehouse. Then I drove home, and Molly cussed me out good for driving, as she felt a half blind man with no license driving all over hell with a toad in a bucket could be a serious threat to the wellbeing of the Buick, which she was awfully fond of.

—Well, do you want to get rid of the damned toad? I says, or don't you?

—I want to get rid of the toad, she says. I just don't want to lose the Buick.

And Wendell Willkie, he looks at me from his cage, and he says, Give me a big kiss, honey.

I told him to go screw himself.

Well, the next morning, there was the damned toad sitting on the bathroom scale. So I bent down to have a good look at him, to see if it was the one with the lipstick on his back, and

I thought I saw a lipstick mark, but it seemed like I'd put it on the right side, and this mark was on the left side. Then I had to think, was it my right side or the toad's right side, and I got all confused, so his time I took the lipstick and I painted a little hat on his head. Then I put him in the bucket and before Molly could get up and stop me I got in the Buick and drove that toad damn near half way to the Pennsylvania line.

Well, I was just about to stop and let the toad out, when I heard a siren, and there come a police car up behind me, so I pulled over, and it was the Sheriff, Big John Bellezzi, a tough old Italian feller, and a very big man, not somebody you ever would want to tangle with, and he says, Cletis, I thought you promised me you wasn't going to drive any more.

And I says, Well, Sheriff, I wasn't going to, but this is kind of an emergency.

And he says, What kind of emergency, Cletis?

And I says, Well, not exactly an emergency, but more in the nature of a family situation.

And he says, What kind of situation, Cletis?

And I says, Well, Sheriff, it's sort of personal.

And he says, What you got in that bucket, Cletis?

And I says, Well, Sheriff, there's a toad in that bucket.

And he says, What are you doing driving around at six o'clock in the morning, half way to East Liverpool, with a toad in a bucket, Cletis?

And I says, It's kind of a long story, Sheriff.

And he's looking at that toad, and he says, Cletis, you know somebody drew a little hat on that toad's head?

And I says, Yes, Sheriff, I know, I drew that hat on his head, with Molly's lipstick.

And he says, Why did you draw a little hat on that toad's head, Cletis?

And I says, So I could tell if it was the same toad.

And he says, The same toad as what, Cletis?

And I says, The same toad as the rest of them, that's been weighing themselves on the bathroom scale in the mornings, and gettin the Little Old Man in an uproar, so Molly can't pee.

And Big John Bellezzi looks at me, and he looks at the toad, and he says, Get out of the car, Cletis.

And I says, All right. I got to get rid of this toad, anyway.

And he says, Give me the bucket, Cletis. I'll get rid of that toad for you.

And I says, Don't hurt it, Sheriff.

And he says, I'm not going to hurt it, Cletis. And he dumps the toad out of the bucket in the ditch, and it hops off into the weeds.

I hope that's the last I see of that damned toad, I says.

Me to, says the Sheriff.

So he takes me home and makes me swear not to drive the Buick no more, and Molly gives me a good hour's worth of screaming, and the Little Old Man hides under the couch, and the rest of the day is not a very happy experience. But you know, I can't stop thinking about that toad. I mean, this is a very perplexing thing.

In the first place, I still don't know how the hell any toad could get into that bathroom, since it was all sealed up every-where because of the rats. And in the second place, I don't know how that toad could have got back in the house after I put him out. And in the third place, I don't know how he could have got back from half way to the Crab Apple Whorehouse. And in the fourth place, I don't know how that lipstick mark could have moved from one side of the toad to the other. So I got to thinking, maybe this isn't any accident. Maybe this is some kind of a sign. Maybe it means something. Maybe all this has some kind of larger significance I just can't quite see. It just got me feeling all philosophical about the nature of life, and who we are, and how we can be sure of who we are, and who everybody else is, and how mysterious the universe re-ally is, and what a privilege it is just to be here trying to figure it all out.

So what I did was, I got me a bottle of Jim Beam and I sat up all night on the toilet. I thought, well, if that goddamned toad comes back, at least I'm gonna see how the hell he gets in here. Well, I must have dozed off about four-thirty in the morning, because when Molly opened up the bathroom door at six-forty-five we scared the living shit out of each other. But there wasn't any toad. The toad was gone.

I suppose I should have been satisfied. I mean, I'd got what I wanted. The toad was gone. But I wasn't satisfied. I felt uneasy. I felt sad. I felt a great sense of emptiness, of genuine loss. I guess I missed the toad. I guess I missed the excitement of having such a complex problem to solve. And then I started worrying about what happened to him. Did he get squashed on the road? Did he get swallowed by a black snake? A lot of terrible things can happen to a toad in the wild, you know. I started to feel guilty. I felt like I'd betrayed a friend. I felt like this toad had come into my life as a kind of a symbol of something, of how there was more going on in the universe than I could ever hope to understand. And I'd just turned my back on him, got rid of him, turned him away. Well, I got over it.

But three days later, I was sitting at the table drinking my coffee with Wendell when I heard the screaming and the yapping, and Molly come into the kitchen and says, Well, I hope you're happy now. Your damned toad is back.

Well, I went in to have a look, and sure enough, sitting there on the bathroom scale, there was this big, fat old toad. So I bent down to have a look and see if I could make out that little hat I'd painted on his head with the lipstick, but all I could see was kind of a stain there, a little darkish splotch, but I wasn't sure if it was just the toad's natural coloring, or if maybe the lipstick had kind of washed off in the rain. But in my heart, I didn't really care. I decided there are just some things man wasn't meant to understand, like why we're born, and why we suffer, and why we die, and whether there's a life after death, and why anybody wants to watch that plate spinning feller on the Ed Sullivan Show. Sometimes a little mystery in a person's life is the best damned thing about it.

So I went back out to the kitchen, and I says, Molly, you better get used to having that damned toad sitting on the bathroom scale in the morning, because I'm not messing with him no more. And if you don't like it, you're just going to have to learn to pee in the garage.

(He drinks his coffee. The light fades on him and goes out.)

END OF PLAY

THE MALEFACTOR'S BLOODY REGISTER

CHARACTERS

Mary Jones
Mary Mitchell
Mary Clifford
John Brownrigg

SETTING

A bare stage with one lamp suspended above the three
girls, making a small circle of light in which they
huddle together.

"The long scene of torture in which this inhuman woman kept
the innocent object of her remorseless cruelty, ere she finished
the long-premeditated murder, engaged the interest of the
superior ranks, and roused the indignation of the populace more
than any criminal occurrence in the whole course of our
melancholy narratives."
—*The Newgate Calendar,* or, *Malefactor's Bloody Register*

THE MALEFACTOR'S BLOODY REGISTER

(Sound of a ticking clock in darkness. Then the light comes up on three girls in white nightgowns, MARY JONES, MARY MITCHELL and MARY CLIFFORD, huddled together on the floor in a circle of light made by a lamp suspended above them. JOHN BROWNRIGG is a young man who lurks in the dark just out of the light. He has an ugly looking stick which he will use later to poke the suspended light and make it swing back and forth.)

MARY JONES. A poor girl of the precinct of White Friars in the year 1765, put apprentice to Mrs Brownrigg, who received pregnant women to lie in privately.

MARY MITCHELL. I was treated with some civility at first.

MARY CLIFFORD. One lived. One died. One was lost. Which was which?

JOHN BROWNRIGG. My mother being a kindly woman.

MARY MITCHELL. But one day Mary Jones spilled a bit of honey.

JOHN BROWNRIGG. Mother loved honey. To spill your honey is a sin. She taught me that.

MARY MITCHELL. And Mrs Brownrigg laid her across two chairs in the kitchen and whipped her until her arm was too weary to whip her further.

MARY CLIFFORD. One lived. One died. One was lost. Which was which?

MARY MITCHELL. Sometimes, when she'd done whipping her, she'd throw water on her.

JOHN BROWNRIGG. The way the nightgown clung to her body was sinful, and the way she trembled in the cold. Her shuddering in the cold.

MARY MITCHELL. And sometimes she'd dip her head in a bucket of water.

MARY CLIFFORD. Hanging naked by the wrists, swaying back and forth with the whipping. Back and forth.

JOHN BROWNRIGG. My mother having borne sixteen children, and having practiced midwifery, appointed by the overseer of the poor to care for women taken in labor in the workhouse, and performed her duties always to the entire satisfaction of her employers.

MARY MITCHELL. For our sins. Whipped for our sins.

MARY JONES. Which sins?

MARY CLIFFORD. We don't know.

MARY MITCHELL. Spilling the honey.

MARY JONES. An apprentice is one who is taken in, to learn a trade.

JOHN BROWNRIGG. Having passed the early part of her life in the service of private families, was married to James Brownrigg, a plumber, who took a house in Flower-de-Luce Court, Fleet Street.

MARY JONES. One of the children of the Foundling Hospital.

MARY CLIFFORD. One lived. One died. One was lost. Which was which?

MARY MITCHELL. The room appointed for Mary Jones to sleep in adjoined the passage leading to the street door.

MARY JONES. And as I had received many wounds upon my head, shoulders, and various parts of my body, I determined not to bear such treatment any longer, if I could effect my escape.

JOHN BROWNRIGG. Sixteen children, of which I was the last to come through that sacred bloody portal.

MARY MITCHELL. Observing that the key was left in the street door when the family went to bed, Mary Jones opened it cautiously one morning, and escaped into the street.

JOHN BROWNRIGG. Fecundity. The evil of fecundity.

MARY JONES Thus freed from my horrid confinement, I staggered about in the street, repeatedly inquiring my way to the foundling hospital.

MARY CLIFFORD. One lived. One died. One was lost. Which was which?

MARY JONES. There I was examined naked by a surgeon, who found my wounds to be of a most alarming nature, and the governors of the hospital ordered their solicitor, Mr Plumbtree, to write to James Brownrigg, threatening prosecution, if he did not give a proper reason for the severities exercised towards the child.

MARY CLIFFORD. A proper reason.

JOHN BROWNRIGG. God's midwife. His handmaiden.

MARY MITCHELL. But no notice of this having been taken—

MARY JONES. No notice.

MARY MITCHELL. And the governors of the hospital thinking it imprudent—

MARY CLIFFORD. Imprudent.

MARY MITCHELL. To indict at common law—

MARY JONES. Common law.

MARY MITCHELL. The girl was discharged.

MARY JONES. Discharged.

JOHN BROWNRIGG. Bloody discharge. Hideous. What a mess.

MARY MITCHELL. But I remained.

MARY JONES. At night I go there and look in the windows.

MARY CLIFFORD. I have seen a face at the window.

MARY JONES. Outside looking in.

MARY MITCHELL. Until, after a year of such torture, I too escaped from the house—

MARY CLIFFORD. One lived. One died. One was lost. Which was which?

MARY MITCHELL. But was soon apprehended by young John Brownrigg, their son.

JOHN BROWNRIGG. We have missed you at home, Mary.

(He reaches out his stick from the darkness and pokes the lamp very gently. It sways back and forth, creaking and casting odd shadows.)

MARY MITCHELL. And was treated with increased cruelty afterwards.

MARY JONES. Watching in the window. Watching.

MARY MITCHELL. And in the meantime, the overseers of the precinct of White Friars, in their wisdom, bound also one Mary Clifford to the Brownriggs.

MARY CLIFFORD. One lived. One died. One was lost. Which was which?

MARY MITCHELL. This Mary Clifford being so fair and delicate, I knew she would get worse than the others.

MARY CLIFFORD. Tied up naked and beaten with a hearth-broom, a horsewhip, or a cane, until I could not speak.

MARY JONES. Looking in the dirty window.

MARY MITCHELL. This poor girl having a natural infirmity—

JOHN BROWNRIGG. Pretty Mary Clifford wets herself in the night.

MARY MITCHELL. The mistress would not permit her to lie in a bed, but placed her on a mat, in a coal hole that was remarkably cold.

JOHN BROWNRIGG. I must make a notation of this in my book, said Mother.

MARY MITCHELL. But after a time, only a sack and a quantity of straw formed her bed.

JOHN BROWNRIGG. For she kept a blood-spattered book in which she recorded the smallest incidents regarding the servant girls, which is evidence of the great affection which she bore for them.

MARY MITCHELL. During her confinement in this wretched situation, she had nothing to subsist on but bread and water, and her covering, during the night, consisted only of her own clothes, so that sometimes she lay almost perished with cold.

JOHN BROWNRIGG. Shuddering, all shuddering on the floor. The cold is the breath of God. It teaches us about his love. About the true nature of God's love.

(He pushes the lamp with the stick again, a little harder.)

MARY CLIFFORD. Once I broke open a cupboard, in search of food, but found it empty. I drank water from a puddle in the cellar.

MARY MITCHELL. Mrs Brownrigg, seeing the broken cupboard, caused Mary Clifford to remain naked a whole day, while she repeatedly beat her with the butt end of a whip, a jack-chain fixed around her neck, the end of which was fastened to the yard door, and pulled as tight as possible without strangling her.

MARY CLIFFORD. Around my throat. Around my throat. The fingers of God. I hear him whispering to me in the coal hole at night, pitch black and shuddering, his fingers.

MARY MITCHELL. Kept naked for days at a time, and so frequently beaten our heads and shoulders appeared as one general sore, and when a plaster was applied, the skin peeled away with it.

MARY CLIFFORD. It is a test, I said to myself. All life is a test of our love for God.

MARY MITCHELL. When Mrs Brownrigg was in ill spirits, she would tie our hands with a cord, and draw them up to a water pipe, which ran across the ceiling in the kitchen. But that giving way, she desired her husband to fix a hook in the beam, through which a cord was drawn, and, our arms being extended, she used to horsewhip us until blood flowed at every stroke, and she was weary.

JOHN BROWNRIGG. Mary Clifford. Put up a half-tester bedstead.

MARY CLIFFORD. I beg your pardon, sir?

JOHN BROWNRIGG. A half-tester bedstead. Mother says to put up a half-tester bedstead.

MARY CLIFFORD. I don't know what that is, sir.

JOHN BROWNRIGG. Do I hear you refuse to put up a half-tester bedstead?

MARY CLIFFORD. I don't refuse. I don't know how. I don't know what it is.

JOHN BROWNRIGG. *(Pushing the lamp harder with his stick, the light now swinging madly back and forth, creaking.)* This is grounds for a serious discussion, Mary.

(He begins walking in a circle around the girls, at the edge of the light, poking at the lamp with his stick now and then to make it swing more and more.)

MARY MITCHELL. Mrs Brownrigg would seize her by the cheeks, and force the skin down violently with her fingers, causing the blood to gush from her eyes.

MARY CLIFFORD. There was a kind French lady, lodged in the house, and I told her of our treatment, and begged her help.

JOHN BROWNRIGG. Now, this is the nature of God's world, Mary.

MARY CLIFFORD. But when she heard of it, Mrs Brownrigg came at me like a crow, and cut my tongue in two places with a pair of scissors. I never spoke again.

MARY MITCHELL. On the morning of July 13th, Mrs Brownrigg ordered Mary Clifford to strip to the skin, then hung her up and beat her till the blood ran down, then made her wash herself in a tub of cold water, while I watched. She beat her again while she was washing herself. Five times she beat her on this day.

JOHN BROWNRIGG. There are four ways to cope with God's world, Mary.

MARY MITCHELL. Her wounds began to show signs of mortification.

JOHN BROWNRIGG. Die. Go mad. Fight him. Or join him.

MARY JONES. I knocked on the door of the neighbor, Mrs Deacon, and asked her if she did not hear groans and screams from the Brownrigg house, and I begged her to watch, and she took pity on me, a starving girl who lurked in the street, looking in windows, and took me in as a maid.

JOHN BROWNRIGG. I have chosen to join him. And this is the cause of all my happiness.

(He pokes the lamp again. It swings violently back and forth now.)

MARY JONES. When old Mr Brownrigg went to Hampstead on business, and bought a hog, he put it in a covered yard, having a skylight, which it was thought necessary to remove, as a kindness to the animal. Mr Deacon told his servants to look through the window, and I saw the girl there, Mary Clifford, lying naked by the hog. I called the neighbors to see.

MARY CLIFFORD. Faces looking down at me, like angels from heaven. They dropped pieces of dirt down upon my flesh, but I could not speak to them.

MARY JONES. Mr Grundy of the overseers was summoned, and went to the Brownriggs' door and demanded to see Mary. Mary Mitchell was brought. I said it was the wrong Mary. Send for a constable, I said. And I kept at them until they did, and the house was searched, but Mary Clifford was not found. But Mr Grundy took Mary Mitchell out of the house, to the workhouse.

MARY MITCHELL. He stripped off all my clothes. My leathern bodice stuck to the wounds. I screamed. I would not speak until they swore I'd not go back to Brownriggs. Then I told them about Mary Clifford, and how I met her bleeding on the stairs, and where they kept her in a cupboard, covered with old shoes.

MARY JONES. Mr Grundy went back, and despite the threats of the Brownriggs, got Mary Clifford out of the cupboard. Her body was all ulcerated. She could not speak. She was taken to an apothecary, who pronounced her in grave danger.

MARY CLIFFORD. One lived. One died. One was lost. Which was which?

MARY JONES. Brownrigg was arrested then, but wife and son escaped.

JOHN BROWNRIGG. Take the gold watch, John, said Mother, and all the coin.

MARY MITCHELL. Mary Clifford died at Saint Bart's a few days after. The three of them charged with murder.

MARY CLIFFORD. One lived. One died. One was lost. Which was which?

JOHN BROWNRIGG. *(Walking faster around the circle, pushing at the lamp in a kind of frenzy.)* Shifted from place to place in London, bought clothes at the Rag Fair to disguise ourselves, then took lodgings above a chandler's shop, but the chandler read of it in the papers, and there we were taken, Mother and me, wretched together in our filthy room, praying to God for deliverance. Mother weeping and screaming. I never seen her weep before. The bloody little bitches have made my mother weep. It's a sin to make a mother weep.

MARY JONES. Father, mother and son were tried, the mother, after eleven hours, found guilty of murder, but father and son only a misdemeanor, six months.

JOHN BROWNRIGG. On her way to the fatal tree such shrieking at her. Horrible things. People with the faces of demons. Shameful. Where was God then? Where was he then?

MARY MITCHELL. Mrs Brownrigg declared her guilt before all, and acknowledged the justice of her sentence. Then she was strung up, at Tyburn, September the 14th, 1767, her body after put in a hackney coach, and conveyed to Surgeons' Hall, where it was dissected, her skeleton hung on display.

MARY CLIFFORD. One lived. One died. One was lost. Which was which?

JOHN BROWNRIGG. When I got out, I went to visit Mother.

MARY JONES. I stayed in service and married a footman. Children of my own now. Yesterday I thought I saw Mary Mitchell, walking in Rose Alley, but I couldn't be sure.

MARY MITCHELL. One lived, one died, one was lost. Which was which?

MARY JONES. And once I thought I saw her at the Rag Fair, talking to the empty air.

MARY MITCHELL. Come, Mary, we'll get you some nice clothes at the Rag Fair, for your disguise, and no one will suspect that you are dead.

MARY CLIFFORD. One lived. One died. One was lost. Which was which?

JOHN BROWNRIGG. There was Mother, hung up like a sausage, like a Christmas goose at the medical hall. God took all the skin off her and devoured the flesh. I stood and stared at her, trying to understand her gaping grin. And in her face, for just a moment, flickering there, I thought I saw another face, the face of God.

(He is no longer poking at the lamp, and it's begun to swing back and forth more slowly now.)

MARY JONES. At night I tell my children stories, and tuck them in, and watch them sleep.

MARY MITCHELL. Rag fair. The rag fair. No one will know.

MARY CLIFFORD. No one will know.

JOHN BROWNRIGG. I dream of those three at night, and I think of all the times we had. Sweet memories of childhood.

MARY CLIFFORD. One lived. One died. One was lost. Which was which?

JOHN BROWNRIGG. And I think of my mother's face, her face with the flesh on it, and also with it off, and I forgive those girls, for in my mother's visage I have seen the face of God, or one of them, and I know God's love is infinite, and extends even to sinners such as those three girls. But when I dream of the faces, the fleshy face and the bony one, I wonder.

MARY JONES. One lived.

MARY MITCHELL. One died.

MARY CLIFFORD. One was lost.

JOHN BROWNRIGG. Which was which?

(A moment. Then the light goes out. Just the creaking the lamp as it sways back and forth in the darkness.)

END OF PLAY

CAPONE

CAPONE

(Lights up on AL CAPONE, in bathrobe and slippers, at his house at Palm Island, Florida. Perhaps the year is 1946. He is a powerful looking, beefy man in his late forties.)

CAPONE. So I said to her, Honey, you got a nice ass, and I mean that as a compliment. How was I supposed to know the son of a bitch was her brother? Cut my face open with a steak knife. How I got these scars. Lucky Luciano said I should apologize, so I did. What the hell. Guy slices my face open like a salami, I apologize. It was a test. Johnny Torrio left money on the table to see what we'd do. Most kids took it. I didn't. Everything is a test. Johnny didn't smoke, drink, swear or screw around. He was a real gentleman. They shot him in front of his wife. He was like a father to me. My father was a barber from Naples. Never hit me once. He talked to me. The priest put salt in your mouth to cast out demons. Black Hand would snatch up kids in the street and kill them if you didn't pay. Honored Sir, the letter said. Black borders. Daggers and skulls. We all hated them. All decent people hated them. They were sewage. Not that Mulberry Street Bend crowd. I'm talking about Red Hook. Brooklyn. The stink off the Gowanus Canal could make a gargoyle cry. Train tracks up in the air by the schoolhouse window. Loved that girl but she was thirteen and her parents said I was a gangster so I married Mae although she was Irish. What the hell was McSwiggen doing with the damned O'Donnels anyway? Cut them damn near in half. Stupid damned potato eater. Mick firemen stood watching my whore house burn. Couldn't spare the water. Why don't you try and pee on it, Al? Most of them were customers. They say syphilis is a bad thing, but I don't know. Something itching at the brain, like a pretty young whore you can't get off your mind. Dripping in your head like a leaky faucet. Stiffs floating in the green muck slopping at the shore. Sea gulls and rotting weeds. Running liquor at night from New York past the sand dunes with Happy Hoolihan. Pelicans fly across the moon like a picture. Played the harmonica. Sister with the eye patch. Shot Perotta in the stomach. What a mess. Must have been a bleeder.

Went to Chicago with forty dollars in my pocket. Chicago is the greatest place in the world. You can bribe anybody and you can screw anybody, and it's got the most civic-minded dead people in the country. And it's a working man's city. Even the pimps got a union. Here's what I learned in Chicago: politics is business, and business is violence, and violence is corruption, and corruption is God. A thing I already learned from counting the stiffs floating in the Gowanus Canal. But everything you learn is something you already knew. This is why education is a wonderful thing, although educated people are usually morons. Clarence Darrow used to sit and drink with Caruso at Colosimo's Café. Big Jim was a collector for Hinky Dink McKenna and Bathhouse Coughlin, the two crookedest damned aldermen since pigs was pork. Loved a girl singer named Winter. Left his wife. Love is a beautiful thing. Frankie Yale shot him in the back of the head. Frankie was a Calabrian undertaker with an ice pick, but the biggest crook in Chicago was Big Bill Thompson, who coincidentally also happened to be the mayor. For two bucks, Big Bill Thompson would collect your farts in a bottle. Warren Harding had the right idea—the return to Normalcy. Normalcy is a state of perpetual theft. To get the Irish vote, Big Bill told them he'd uncovered evidence the King of England had secret plans to invade Chicago. I don't know what the fuck the King of England wanted with Chicago, unless he was looking for a pimp. Maybe he wanted his farts collected in a bottle. How can you tell a Chicago judge from a hooker? There are some things a hooker won't do for money. Just slip him a few thousand, he'll send back the ledgers. Screwing at the Blue Goose. Little teenage flapper girl with a spoon around her neck to stuff coke up her nose, take her in the back and screw her until she squeals. Perforated septum. I love the sounds a woman makes. It's like beautiful music to me, when she gets pleasure. It's a religious thing, like opera. Opera is an amazing invention. Pagliacci. Sicilian Vespers. I got a big stack of seventy-eights. Opera is how God talks to us. Opera and naked women. Just don't call me a pimp. Son of a bitch fucking minister burned down my brothel. Newspaper give me shit, but I didn't burn it down. I bought it. That's the problem with religious people, they got no morals.

At the Four Deuces a hooker was two bucks, and for five bucks you could watch two whores do it with each other. We called that a circus. I love show business. Greasy Thumb Guzik with his white slave Mona. Missing a kidney. Jellied calves' feet. But there's nothing like the smell of spaghetti sauce in a house. That's what heaven is, I think. Somebody is always making spaghetti there. I made spaghetti sauce for the reporters once in a big pink apron. Something is eating my brain. I can hear it inside there. Linguine with clam sauce. Johnny Torrio was gonna move his Mama back to Italy so I could take over the rackets. Family is important. My brother Vincenzo was Two-Gun Hart the Prohibition Man. I myself was a used furniture dealer. So Johnny is carrying groceries behind his wife one day. Spaghetti, tomatoes, whatever. Blue Cadillac comes around the corner, Hymie Weiss and Bugs Moran get out of the car with sawed off shotguns. Blasted him twice. Then when he was screaming on the sidewalk, walked up and plugged him in the groin. He was a negotiator but I never had time for that crap. Yap yap yap. Then that fucking judge drives

an army of off duty cops to Cicero and murders my brother
Frank, gunned him down in the street. Handsome Frank, he
never hurt nobody in his life, shot him down like a deer.
Everything changes once you seen your brother in a silver
plated coffin. That fruitcake O'Banion had the whole place
covered in flowers. The cops who killed him watching from
Studebakers. O'Banion's head got away from his hat. The
Gennas bootleg whiskey was full of rats. I hate rats. Rats make
you crazy. Rats inside my head, eating my brain. Linguine
with clam sauce. Shot O'Banion in the flower shop, five in
the guts, one in the eyesocket. Poor Tommy they found stuffed
head first down a well. The water stank is how they found
him. Holy Name Cathedral. Rented a room across from the
flower shop. Hymie Weiss dead on the railroad tracks. Call
me a snake now, you son of a bitch. A thousand fucking shots
into the Hawthorne. What did the stupid son of a bitch expect?
I stood up. Rio tackled me. Get down, boss. It's a trick. A
thousand shots. It was like a fucking shooting gallery. They
made shredded Parmesan out of a innocent family in a car
outside. I paid their doctor bills. Ten thousand bucks. I try to
do the right thing.

Johnny would have declared a truce and sat down to talk
about it over ravioli, but I figure, a man calls you a snake, start
carving the fucking tombstone. I considered it an act of civic
duty. I supplied them with liquor and helped fight crime by
eliminating criminals from the streets. And everybody drank.
The reporters drank. The cops drank. The fucking politicians
drank like there was no tomorrow. And for some of them there
wasn't. I believe in democracy. I think it's the greatest form of
government. The best way to win an election is to throw all
the Democrats in the basement and beat the living shit out of
them. All my life I been a Republican, and I'm proud of it. In
Chicago, we had a whole slate of candidates, all Republicans.
Republicans make the best criminals because they look so dig-
nified when they're kissing your ass. Howard called me a pimp
so I shot him in the face. Dead with a big grin on the floor.

Everybody in the place was stooping behind the bar, looking for a package of nickels with his head up his ass. Kept our liquor in the basement of the town hall. I kicked the fucking mayor down the town hall steps while the cops watched. I'm just happy to be an American.

So we called this peace conference. Hotel Sherman, across the street form the police chief's office. Big Bill Thompson, Guzik, Lombardo, Bugs Moran, Drucci, Jack Zuta. Big Bill Thompson led an expedition to catch tree-climbing fish. Starred in a rat show, onstage with a cage full of rats and watched them eat each other like a bunch of left handed Irishmen. Told his constituents to burn all their books that were written in English. He was an idiot but we had to bribe him because everybody else was. A bathtub full of money. We all got drunk and sang songs. We were going to shoot you lots of times, says Bugs, but every time we saw you, you had a different woman hanging on you, and we didn't think you were worth wasting a woman over. Very funny man, Bugs. Divided up the city. Worked for a while. Then they took Tony the Greek for a ride. Found him frozen like a fucking popsicle. Cop shot Drucci in the back of a squad car. Woops. My gun musta fell out and went off in his mouth. Cops are not as dumb as Republicans. They had a party for politicians on the river, and there was so much bullshit in one place, the boat sank. Big Bill swam to shore with the rats. Turds float. But everything is a racket. Monopolies. Rigged stocks. Income tax. Shit. Some guy named Elmer. You got an Italian name, a dark complexion, you're a crook. A guy with blue eyes who takes your money, him they call a banker. In my office three pictures on the wall: George Washington, Abraham Lincoln, and Big Bill Thompson the rat show man. I thought it was funny, but nobody got the joke.

We had some fun, though. I conducted Rhapsody in Blue at the Metropole after the Dempsey-Tunny rematch. Cotton Club. Fats Waller. Capone's University of Gutbucket Arts. Long count. A fixed fight is a Barney. Some of the best fights

I ever seen was Barneys. Dempsey was a good friend of mine, but I lost a shitload of money on his fights. And while I was getting my picture took with Jack Sharkey some fucking sportswriter stole my wife's jewelry. Damon Runyon. What a liar. Ask my friend Jake Lingle, who is a dead reporter, which is what I call good news. Jake was okay, but he was on the take, like all writers. Died at the end of a tunnel with a cigar in his teeth and a racing form in his hand. Fucking weasel. Diamond studded belt buckle. Crooked as a hairpin. Always trying to screw the same whore three different ways at the same time. But I didn't do it. I was fishing in Florida. Actually, I was. Bugs Moran did it. If I'd committed half the murders they said I did, the nuns would have come to drag me down to hell a long time ago. And that son of a bitch Billy Sunday was a lousy ballplayer. Couldn't hit the curve ball. Never trust a man who lies for money. You don't believe me, ask my lawyer.

I'd trust Machine Gun Jack McGurn first, and he was a psychopath. McGurn was his Irish boxing name, he was really a Gelotti. Playing golf at Burnham Wood with old Machine Gun Jack. Four guys from out of town, dead with a nickel in their hands, nobody could figure out what it meant, but I knew. When they killed McGurn's dad, he had nickel in his hand. Jack had a short fuse but a long memory, just as soon cut off your head as look at you, but boy, could that son of a bitch handle a putting iron. Me, McGurn, Greasy Thumb Guzik, and Banjo Eyes, excellent body guard, looked like a toad, most annoying son of a bitch I ever met. I could drive a long way but I hooked everything. Should have been a fisherman. McGurn would turn somersaults and walk on his hands. We'd play leap frog and Blind Robin. One guy lays down on the grass and holds the tee in his teeth while the other guys tee off. We musta whacked old Banjo Eyes in the ear a hundred times but he never caught on. Hard of hearing after that. Drove me nuts. Called me a liar once when he thought I said his mother screwed horses, so I pulled my gun out of my golf bag and stuck it half way down his throat, but the caddie was cry ing, so I let him go. We all cheated. One day I picked up the golf bag and my gun fell out and went off and shot me in the groin. Everybody hit the dirt. Golf is a lot more dangerous than bootlegging. Then I was just getting it healed up when a waitress spilled hot coffee on my lap. I almost shot her right there but she was so pretty I decided to be magnanimous and screw her instead. Sweet sixteen. Orgies in the clubhouse. Looked like a picture of hell. I know they play golf in hell. Good times.

My theory is, you don't control a person by screaming at him. That just makes him hate you. What you do is, you look at him and figure out what he wants, how he wants to see himself, and then you let him have that. You let him have that, like a gift. You don't take that from him. And he'll be so relieved you didn't cut his fucking balls off and go bowling with his head, he'll do anything for you. Fear ain't really what you want, see. Fear is the tool you use to get what you want, but fear is like your dick, it works better if you don't use it all the time. Sure, every now and then it don't hurt to cut off somebody's head as a kind of an object lesson, but what you really want is loyalty, like when they did Frankie Yale for killing Jimmy Files. I was fishing at the time, out to dinner with a big fiddle case full of machine guns and gold rimmed dinner plates. Frankie pulls up to a light, Forty-fourth street, Brooklyn, in his nice red Lincoln, looks in his rear view mirror and sees a big black Buick coming up behind him with Scalise, Anselmi, Machine Gun Jack and Killer Burke. He must have had a pretty solid suspicion they wasn't there to say hello. Car was bullet proof but the window glass wasn't. Poor dumb son of a bitch. So this family at a bar-mitzvah party looks up and sees Frankie Yale's big red Lincoln smashing into the front stoop. Door pops open, Frankie flops out like a beautifully dressed piece of swiss cheese with ketchup. His wife ended up sewing pants for a living. Brooklyn. I miss the old neighborhood.

Prosecutor said Italians were criminals by nature. Brutal, dumb, dishonest. Don't know what he thought about Leonardo, Dante, Verdi and Michelangelo. He himself was a stupid, sheep-fucking Swede. Them people don't know shit about meatballs, either. They paid my brother Two-Gun to guard Calvin Coolidge in South Dakota when he wore those Indian feathers on his head. Al Capone's brother guarding the president and nobody knew. I guess Two-Gun wasn't on his fucking index cards. This Swede had everything he knew on index cards. Should have cut his throat with a fucking index card. Greasy Thumb Guzik lived right around the corner from this four-eyed Swedish cocksucker. Their dogs used to take turns screwing each other, just like election time in Chicago. Pineapple in your bread box. Boom. Dumdum bullets in the brain. Head of the Crime Commission came and asked me to keep order so they could have safe elections. Always happy to do my bit. Snowball put out the fuse, but I was the real Mayor of Chicago. A great American success story. Blew off the head of the Police chief. Chicago Heights. Sitting in his parlor, reading the funnies, blamm, no head. Sledge hammers to slot machines, nickles exploding in the air like fireworks, little kids chasing pieces of brain on the floor. You got to love Chicago. But the Feds are like an elephant, they move slow but the shit keeps coming. The Feds are worms eating my brain, little men like gnomes with thick glasses in tiny offices staring at old yellow ledgers spotted with blood. They ate my brother Ralph. Best hot dogs in the world at the six day bicycle races. McGurn loved them. Bugs Moran paid the Gusenberg brothers to knock Jack off. Ambushed him in a phone booth. Ventilated him pretty good. Thought he was dead. But old Jack was like Frankenstein, you could kill him but he'd keep coming back in the next movie. Let's get the bastards all at once in their fucking garage, Al, he says. But I didn't know nothing about it at the time. I was in Miami looking at a coconut plantation.

Valentine's Day. Cold. Windy. Eighteen degrees in the morning. McGurn was screwing his girl Louise. Killer Burke, Egan's Rats, Scalise, Anselmi, stole a police car and some uniforms. Purple Gang was lookouts. In the garage was the Gusenberg brothers, Weinshank, Kashellek, Heyer, May, and

Schwimmer, eye doctor with a red carnation. German shepherd tied to a pipe. Line them up against the wall, took their guns, no problem. Thought it was a police raid. Dog howling. Lucky son of a bitch Bugs was always late, saw the police car and walked right on by. Frankie Gusenberg had twenty-two bullet holes in him, cops asked him, who shot you, Frankie? Who shot you? Nobody, he says. Nobody shot me. Twenty-two bullet holes. Musta been a bad hunting accident. Five guys with their heads blown open laying there in the garage, puddles of gore, everybody taking pictures. German shepherd still tied up, going crazy, lunging and snarling. Nobody would go near the dog. Cops were gonna shoot him, but somebody let him go instead. Tore off down the street like a bat out of hell. I like dogs. Dogs are good people. O'Rourke said after walking around in that garage he had more brains on his feet than he did in his head. In his case it was true. Only Capone kills like that, Bugs said. But I was in Florida, fishing. They got Burke but McGurn married his blonde alibi. Happy Valentine's Day from Al to Bugs. You got to love your work to really do well at it.

But there was a rumor Scalise and Anselmi went over to Hop Toad the Sicilian, so me and Frankie Rio faked an argument. I let him hit me in the face to make it look good. Next day, sure enough, there was Scalise and Anselmi come to see Frankie, offering to knock me off for him. So we put together a big banquet for them in Hammond. Everybody got drunk. Tied them to their chairs, just for laughs, and then I beat their fucking heads in with a baseball bat. I had a pretty good swing in them days. I coulda been another Babe Ruth. So the boys in New York start to get worried maybe I'm just a little bit out of control. On account of the garage full of brains and my recent attempts to improve my swing using the heads of these two Sicilian goombahs as baseballs and so forth, so they call this big conference in Atlantic City. Everybody was there. Lucky Luciano. Dutch Schulz. Albert Anastasia, a real sweetheart of a guy. Lepke. Lansky. And Johnny Torrio, who amazingly enough was still not dead, and they want to move me out, make him head of the whole fucking national organization. And this thing is eating my brains. So I paid these two Philadelphia cops to arrest me. I thought jail would be the safest place, but I swear to god, in Philly you actually got to bribe somebody to get arrested. But the cheese steak is very good, and I recommend it, although the grease drip is murder on a pinstripe suit. Philadelphia is not such a bad place if the alternative is laying face down in a puddle ditch with a hole in your head and your dick sliced off like a pepperoni stick.

And speaking of dicks, Eliot Ness was tapping my brother's phone. Ness was a drunk named after a woman writer called George. Look who's here, said the whores at Cozy Corners. It's Richard Barthlemess. Greasy Thumb Guzik at the Wabash Hotel. Ness up a fucking telephone pole. What do you hear from Snorky? Ten ton truck with a fucking battering ram to the brewery. We called it Eliot Ness's artificial schlong. Always striking a pose, like a fucking department store mannikin on the cover of *Time* magazine, a place where a great many other criminals, pimps, and murderers from all walks of life have also appeared. Fucking sheriff threw my watch in the toilet. Snitches coming out of the woodwork like roaches. O'Hare had this mechanical rabbit we used at the dog track, it could shit diamonds. But everybody's got a weakness. Fred was afraid of cockroaches. So they put him in a room swarming with these big, fat roaches until he said he'd give evidence against me. Hell, he'd have testified against Shirley Temple just to get the fuck out of that room full of cockroaches. And me with my own Al Capone Soup Kitchen. I fed more people in the Depression than all those rich pigs put together. It's a fact. You can look it up. Best beef stew I ever had in my life. Called me a reptile in front of all those corset manufacturers. And in the year 1930, I was on the list of the ten most outstanding persons in the world. It was Lindbergh, Herbert Hoover, Henry Ford, Einstein, Mussolini, Gandhi and me. People loved me. I was like Florence Nightingale, only with a machine gun and lasagna.

So I get this Irish guy to write the story of my life, to contradict all these lies about me they're spreading, and the waiter brings this fucking artificial Parmesan, smells like a bull farted on it. Lucky I didn't scoop out his eyeballs with the soup spoon. Fucking bad cheese. Where does this guy get off, embarrassing me in front of this fucking Irish four eyed autobiographer? I mean, I try to be a civilized person, but never serve an Italian bad cheese. Do you know Murray the Hump was a Welshman? Since when is a Welshman a mobster? The only Welsh gangster who ever lived. Not that I'm prejudiced. I treated everybody equal—Irish, Jews, blacks. I didn't care. This is America. I can work with anybody. Except for the Sicilians, they're a bunch of fucking lunatics. But I even hired Sicilians, because no matter what you say about them, they make great murderers. Of course, I did have to beat their fucking brains in with a Louisville Slugger, but still, you can't say I didn't give them a chance. In America everybody should get a chance, no matter where they come from or who they are. This is what I believe. Just don't serve me any of that fucking horsefart cheese.

So Eliot Ness is peeking in windows and listening at keyholes and chasing beer barrels all over Chicago and calling me Snorky like he knew me or something, claimed he found a bomb under his hood. Personally I think he put it there himself. The man loved publicity like a pig loves shit. Bribe the fucking jurors. Went to the Northwestern game with McGurn and got booed and chased out by Boy Scouts. Fucking Boy Scouts. I coulda taken those guys, but I figured they all had mothers. And for what? A roulette wheel and a chuck-a-luck outfit? What the fuck is chuck-a-luck? A parrot cage and a dice roll. At my trial I enjoyed playing hide and seek in the Federal building, which is like a kind of a maze, you know? Like life, or a woman. Rain pouring down. Unlawful possession. Shuffled his feet like he was running a sewing machine. Edward G. Robinson came to the trial to study me. My lawyer brought in bookies to prove I gambled away all my money.

Damon Runyon was cracking up in the back, he thought it was funny. Pen-pushing little weasel. Pretty funny guy, though. Then my lawyer, that classic, he defends me to the jury by talking about the Punic Wars. The fucking Punic Wars. My lawyer, who I was paying enough money to feed half the people in Naples, was standing there speaking Latin to these old Protestant farmers and bean eaters. Carthage must be destroyed, he said. My client is Carthage, he says. And the prosecutors are Cato. What the fuck was he talking about? Who the fuck was that supposed to impress? And the prosecutors they tell the jury I ain't Robin Hood. No, and I ain't Friar fucking Tuck and I ain't fucking Tinker Belle either. What the hell is the matter with lawyers, anyway? Are they all nuts? It was like I thought I was at my trial but I woke up in the middle of a fucking fairy tale. I don't know what the fuck Robin Hood and the Punic Wars got to do with my income tax or what goes on under Wacker Avenue. Maybe somebody can explain that to me. Maybe somebody can explain to me why I'm a criminal and lawyers and politicians and bankers and generals can lie and steal and kill every fucking day of their lives and get away with it. You don't suppose my real crime was being an ugly Italian kid from Brooklyn, do you? Some big crime I committed. I sold people beer. Every fucking person in that courtroom had had some of my beer in his life, except the ones who only drink fucking Frog wine. Eleven years in jail I got for this. Carthage must be destroyed. Jesus Fucking Christ.

The Chicago jail wasn't so bad. I had a butler there. Bread and butter, kidney stew. Bon Bon Allegretti brought me lots of whores. Then they sent me to Atlanta. Where's the broads and booze now, fat boy? Screaming ignorant rednecks. Shoe factory eight hours a day. Warden won't let me have the photographs my wife sent. Overpaid dumb bastard shysters. Al Capone a fucking cobbler in Atlanta. A peach cobbler. Smuggling in snow inside tennis balls. You open up the tennis balls and white birds fly out. And they cut up God and put him inside meat balls. They were all on the run by then. Dillinger dyed his eyebrows black, but they plugged him coming out of the movies. At Alcatraz, cons would go nuts on a regular basis. One guy found an ax and started chopping off his own fingers. Me and Machine Gun Kelly and two hundred killers. It was like the University of Hell. Island of the Pelicans. They retyped all our letters so I couldn't smell my wife. Every day I'd go see Pussyfoot, the warden. He was like God, he always said no. Feeding shirts into the mangle, it kept eating them and eating them. Asshole threw a bench at me so they put me in the dungeon. Al Capone and his orchestra. I played the banjo. Machine Gun Kelly on drums. I switched to the mandolin, but the son of a bitch was blowing his saxophone right in my ear, so I decided to see how far his instrument could be shoved up his ass. Nights I put my head under the blanket and cried. Cowboys stabbed me in the back eight times with barber shears. Put Lucas in solitary for six months, went nuts. Bug ugly. Creepy Karpis screwed Ma Barker. Three Fingers White got his throat cut. I dream about it sometimes. Fresh Italian sausage. Look at their faces through the peep holes. Went wacky in the kitchen. Vomit on the floor. Bug in my head. Paresis.

My son come to see me at Alcatraz. I tried to be a good father, but who knows how to do that? He's grown up now. He's a fine person. Went to Notre Dame with the rich boys. Me, I went to the bug cage with Bughouse Janaway, terror of the Ozarks. Boy, was that guy screwed up. Reached in his chamber pot one day and threw a big handful of shit at me. So what is a gentleman supposed to do under those circumstances, I ask you? So I reached into my own chamber pot, which was also full, and we had this gigantic screaming shit fight. There was shit everywhere. He was laughing. This guy was nuts. Then I was laughing, too. We were both nuts, what the hell. I think maybe Bughouse Carl also had something eating the inside of his head, and we kind of saw that in each other, and it was like finding your long lost brother, you know what I mean? Well, maybe you had to be there. All I know is, throwing shit at Carl Janeway was the most fun I had since the whores stopped coming. So this kind of alarmed the warden and he said they'd let me out if I agreed to rat on Johnny Torrio, who still wasn't dead yet. So I spoke to the Lord about it, and this little voice in my head told me it didn't make any fucking difference. So I talked for twelve days about how William Randolph Hearst framed me because he killed this guy on a boat with a nickelodeon and told Jack Dempsey to bring me to the beach house where I was forced to witness disgusting sexual acts and they said stand up if you feel the need of a personal savior so I stood up and everybody else sat down which is more or less the story of my life in a nutshell and since lucky for Johnny Torrio very little of it made any damned sense whatsoever, they couldn't use it, but they sent him to Leavenworth anyway, and put out word that I ratted on him, but I never did. He was a gentleman from White Plains, and I was the boy who didn't take the money. I was living in Hell at the time, throwing shit at Carl Janeway. What are we talking about? It doesn't matter.

When they let me out, the lake was frozen, and there was fog and sea gulls and pelicans. After malaria treatment in the Caucasus I retired here to Florida where I own a shit factory and teach greyhounds to build chairs. Play pinochle with the boys. I think the bastards cheat, but I can't be sure because of all this jelly in my head. So who's the smart guy now? Huh? Who's the smart guy? My best body guard is a fox terrier. I got beautiful grand-children. I like to buy them presents. Today we read a book about these two hippopotamuses which I thought was pretty good.

Bugs Moran finally got old Jack McGurn, shot him in a bowling alley the day before Valentine's Day, tied a poem to his toe about how at least you haven't lost your trousers. They shot Frank Nitti in the neck but he lived, then blew his own brains out. Frank always said, if you want a job done right, do it yourself. The Feds said he deserved it, but nobody deserves anything. Everybody is crooked. Everybody is a lie. Nobody is legit. Eliot Ness wanted to be a fucking movie star. I'm more honest than most people you salute to. You think the guy who runs your bank is not a criminal? He smiles at you but he takes your money, don't he? And acts like he's doing you a big favor, too. Cornelius Vanderbilt came to see me once, took a high and mighty attitude. I says, you live on Fifth Avenue and sail around in a big fucking yacht while millions of people sleep on benches and live in flop houses. So who the hell are you to look down your nose at me? Did I come see you? And what's the fucking Income Tax but organized robbery? You don't pay, you go to jail. That's extortion. The guys that rob the bank are the poor crooks. The guys that run the bank, they're the rich crooks. The way you tell the difference is, the poor guys are in jail. The rich guys don't need guns because you're so fucking stupid you walk up and stand in line to give them your money.

Paul Muni played me in the movie. George Raft cut out paper dolls. It was a lie about my sister, though. I don't know where the hell they got that. These Hollywood people are sick. Much more dangerous than gangsters. Wiped out Boris Karloff in a bowling alley just like Machine Gun Jack. Art imitates death, I read someplace. Also I was in Dick Tracy. The world is yours. Then you die, and the writers get you, and cut you up into paper dolls. Writers are like hyenas. Crows. They rip off these pieces of flesh one after the other until there's nothing left of what you were, like this thing eating my brain. I was walking in the leaves with a young blond girl the last time before they took me to the place where they ate my brain. Naked in bed she was so perfect I almost didn't want to touch her. I didn't want to spoil how beautiful it was to look at her. Do you know what I mean? I dream about her sometimes. But this place is not so bad here. I wrestle on the floor with the kids. At night I listen to the palm trees rubbing up against the house. It's nice, you know? And we got pelicans.

(The light fades on him and goes out.)

END OF PLAY

NOTEBOOK: CAPONE

Folklore records that the pelican loves its young so dearly it pecks open its own breast to nourish them with its blood. It is a very ancient symbol of Christ and the blood of Communion. The pelican is also one of the most important symbols in alchemy, and the antithesis of the raven. King Lear speaks of his pelican daughters—they are cannibals who feed upon him. My first play, *Pelican Daughter*, connects this imagery in *King Lear* with 'The Pelican Chorus,' a poem by Edward Lear in which the daughter of the pelicans runs off to the Great Gromboolian Plain, with the king of the cranes, and a later play, *The Great Gromboolian Plain*, continues this father and lost daughter theme. The father is the tormented creator, the daughter his beloved but inevitably lost creation. In the context of this play, Alcatraz is the island of the pelicans, and it is there that Capone, like Lear, goes thoroughly mad, although the progression of his illness has of course taken place over many years. Capone has created this nightmare kingdom, this gangster empire in Chicago, as dear to him as Britain is to Lear, and in the end his creation inevitably destroys him. Also like Lear, there is a kind of calm after the storm (the climax of Capone's storm is probably the excrement fight with the mad inmate Bughouse Carl Janaway, a kind of double—remember that Lear needs to wipe his hand before giving it to another, as it smells of mortality), Capone's calm being his peaceful end on Palm Island, playing with his grandchildren, thinking of the young blond girl he didn't want to touch because he'd spoil her beauty, and looking at the pelicans.

His favorite operas were Leoncavallo's *Pagliacci* and several by Verdi: *Aida, La Forza del Destino, Rigoletto,* and *I Vespri Siciliani*, (The Sicilian Vespers), which concerns the uprising which gave birth to the Mafia. Capone saw his life in operatic terms, himself as bigger than life tragic hero, fighting the forces of prejudice and corruption to make a kingdom for himself and a safe haven for his family and friends. These operas were the score he heard in his head as he moved through the movie of his life. And the bigotry and corruption of the hypocritical WASP establishment which he managed to conquer for a time were real. Italians were treated like dirt. They were not allowed into the private WASP world of power and money. From Capone's point of view, all his activities were justified by the prejudice, hypocrisy and corruption of the establishment he was struggling to enter and ultimately become. Ambition, syphilis and time turned his bad temper and capacity for violence into the grotesque brutality of the latter parts of his reign in Chicago.

He loved to cook and to eat Italian food, which is perhaps the central metaphor for family and affirmation of life in Italian-American culture. He liked to talk. He liked to eat. His mind is full of images of devouring, his brain being eaten, his life being devoured by the Feds. He runs a soup kitchen. Linguine and clam sauce, ocean images, water images are related to this. Sauce, wine, blood, ocean, water, bootleg liquor. The blood of the pelican, and ocean bird. Swimming with the fishes. When somebody is murdered, Al is always fishing in Florida. His friend found dead at the bottom of a well. Those are pearls that were his eyes.

Capone's University of Gutbucket Arts: his imaginary orchestra, Big Al conducting Gershwin at the Metropole after the Dempsey-Tunney rematch. Gutbucket: a receptacle for offal in a slaughterhouse. Al conducts like a butcher. He is also the maestro who orchestrates the symphony of butchery in Chicago. His fiddle case is full of gold-rimmed dinner plates and machine guns.

Valentine's day is full of blood. The heart is full of blood. McGurn is screwing his girl Louise. Love and death. Sports was one way Italians got into the mainstream. Babe Ruth and Joe DiMaggio. Al slaughters Scalise and Anselmi with a baseball bat at dinner. He is the ultimate power hitter. Sex, athletic prowess, and violence mixed with love. The sliced pepperoni stick. Ness is up a telephone pole, Ness uses a giant battering ram, all the women love Ness. This is a jungle animal fight for dominance, for women, for control of the herd.

The courtroom, like the legal system, is a labyrinth. He likes playing hide and seek in it with his bodyguards, like a child, but once you step into this labyrinth, you can never find your way out again, and there is a monster waiting at the center to devour you, like the syphilis at the center of his brain. Everybody is crooked, like the labyrinth. Everybody is a lie. Truth is a lie, Picasso said.

In the end, he has been transformed into a mythological figure in the movies, Paul Muni and Edward G. Robinson. He has become a character in Dick Tracy. He is food for writers, who are hyenas, crows, carrion eaters. The man himself is lost, his brain eaten away, and he is a child again, wrestling on the floor with his grandchildren, playing with his dog, listening to the palm trees rub against the house, dreaming about a young blond girl. And they have pelicans.

Don Nigro has written over 180 plays, 86 or which are published by Samuel French in 26 volumes. Produced in 48 states, in London, Oxford & elsewhere in England; Edinburgh & Glasgow, Scotland; Munich & Freiburg, Germany; in Bombay, Calcutta and Madras, India; and in Canada, Iceland, Australia, South Africa, Hungary, Mexico, Hong Kong & Bermuda, his plays include THE SIN-EATER (Actors Theatre of Louisville); CINCINNATI (Edinburgh Festival, Scotland; Juilliard School, NY; SpielArt in Freiburg & Munich); GROTESQUE LOVESONGS (WPA Theatre, NY; Colony Studio Theatre, Los Angeles); SEASCAPE WITH SHARKS AND DANCER (Oregon Shakespeare Festival; Southwark Playhouse, London; Hudson Guild Theatre, NY); LUCIA MAD (Currican Theatre, NY; Theatre X, Milwaukee; Open Stage, Pittsburgh, Washington Stage Guild, DC; Tinfish Theatre, Chicago); LURKER (Manhattan Class Company, NY); SPECTER (Samuel Beckett Theatre, NY; John Houseman Theatre, NY); NECROPOLIS (The Met Theatre in Hollywood); THE GIRLHOOD OF SHAKESPEARE's HEROINES (A Company of Angels, Hollywood; Porthouse Theatre, Ohio; Circle Rep Lab, NY; the University of Natal in Durban, South Africa); MARINER (London School of the Arts); ROBIN HOOD (Marin Shakespeare Company); THE GREAT GROMBOOLIAN PLAIN (Shadowbox Cabaret, Columbus); THE DAUGHTERS OF EDWARD D. BOIT (People's Light & Theatre Company); DEAD MEN'S FINGERS & NOTES FROM THE MOATED GRANGE (Teatro la Gruta in Mexico City); SCARECROW (Theatre/Theatre in Hollywood); RAVENSCROFT (Pendulum Theatre Company, Chicago); THE CURATE SHAKESPEARE AS YOU LIKE IT (Sacramento Theatre Company; Oldcastle Theatre, Orlando Shakespeare Festival); NIGHTMARE WITH CLOCKS (Triangle Theatre Company, NY); PENDRAGON (Idaho Shakespeare Festival); CINDERELLA WALTZ (Vortex Theatre Company & at Ubu Rep in NY); TOMBSTONE (Love Creek Productions, NY); GENESIS, BONEYARD & others at The Present Company in NY & MADELINE NUDE IN THE RAIN PERHAPS and others by OCC Rep in their Nigro Play Festival

Nigro was born in Ohio, has a B.A. in English from Ohio State, an M.F.A. in Dramatic Arts from the Playwrights Workshop at the University of Iowa, and has taught at Ohio State, the University of Massachusetts, Indiana State, the University of Iowa, and Kent State. He's won grants from the National Endowment for the Arts (for FISHER KING), the Mary Roberts Rinehart Foundation (for TERRE HAUTE), and the Ohio Arts Council, has twice been a finalist for the National Repertory Theatre Foundation's National Play Award (for ANIMA MUNDI and THE DARK SONNETS OF THE LADY), and twice been James Thurber Writer in Residence at Thurber House in Columbus. His work has been translated into Italian, German, Russian and Spanish.